SEX DEATH ROCK N ROLL

Short Stories

by

DARREN GORDON SMITH
STACI LAYNE WILSON

This book is a work of fiction. All names, characters, locations, and incidents are products of the author's imagination, or have been used fictitiously. Any resemblance to actual persons living or dead, locales, or events is entirely coincidental.

Copyright © 2015 by Staci Layne Wilson and Darren Gordon Smith

Published by Excessive Nuance in paperback
ISBN-13: 978-0-9675185-4-1

Also available via Kindle

praise for
SEX DEATH ROCK N ROLL

"Anyone can write about rock n roll, but when you get heavy-hitters like Staci Layne Wilson and Darren Gordon Smith applying their combined knowledge of the genre for our entertainment, you know you're in for a rare treat. And what a treat it is. Electrifying, terrifying, and unique. I loved every minute I spent in these dark, deranged worlds. Bring on the sequel!" – Kealan Patrick Burke, Bram Stoker Award-winning Author 'Kin' and 'The Turtle Boy'

"Uniquely nightmarish. There's a touch of Bret Easton Ellis in the stories' surreal mix of anxiety, satire, and obsessive pop music analysis and inventory." – Don Mancini, Saturn-award winning Writer 'Child's Play' films and 'Hannibal' TV series

"Tales of the fantastic blended with the razor kiss of rock n roll." – Tristan Risk, Burlesque Icon 'Little Miss Risk'

"Like a great rock song, this book stays in your head long after you finish it. Funny, macabre and fascinating!" – Jace Anderson, Co-Writer 'Mother of Tears' and 'Fractured' films

"With backstories like these – Wilson's dad is a rockstar (The Ventures), Smith is a musician (*Repo! The Genetic Opera*) – their stories have to be great. And they are!" Bobby Smithe, Author 'Bowie Bible'

"Fiery and fevered scribes Staci Layne Wilson and Darren Smith have delivered an anthology book devoted to rock n roll fuelled short stories which read as lyrical as the songs and music they pay tribute to. With an authentic and un-compromising dedication to musicians from decades past, Wilson and Smith deliver a highly energetic and equally nuanced set of stylish tales of obsession, cynicism, neurosis and rage – all driven by a street sensibility and catapulting from the varied voices of the angry outsider. Not to be missed!" – Lee Gambin, Author 'We Can Be Who We Are: Movie Musicals From the 70s'

contents
SEX DEATH ROCK N ROLL

- - - - - - - - - - - - - - -

About the Authors

FANDOM/PHANTOM
By Smith & Wilson

Side 1, Track 1: *Stayin' Not-Alive*

The best rock stars had the sense to live fast, die young, and leave a good-looking corpse. Jimi Hendrix, Janis Joplin, Jim Morrison, and Russell Aquarius all kicked off at the age of 27. What's more, they went en masse, all shuffling and riffing off the mortal coil by 1971.

But none of them ever came back to life.

At least, not until now.

When she thought about it, *really* thought about it and tried to trace the miracle back to its roots, Alberta thought maybe the whole thing began when she created her first Russell Aquarius fansite and forum. It was just a shitty Geocities thing she cobbled together in the girly bedroom she shared with her younger sister, but it was very popular. She met like-minded fans from all over the world, and for a while, it was awesome.

Then life took over. She graduated high school, got her degree in Computer Science, went to work, moved into her first apartment, took an interest in A.I. (artificial intelligence, not artificial insemination), went back to school for more degrees, and well... eventually, the Russell Aquarius posters were replaced with framed art, and his once-omnipresent image was reduced to a couple of cheap magnets stuck to her fridge.

So what made her start thinking about him again? The plan at first was just to start up another fan page as a hobby. Alberta then figured it would be really cool to make an interactive avatar of Russell on the homepage, so she fed every bit of info about him she could into her PC. All his interviews, text from the dozens of books written about him, thousands of photos, videos of his concerts, recordings of his voice, and of course – all three of his albums (*Furry Freak*, *Peace Mantra*, and *Hi, I'm a Gemini*).

She'd been testing the avatar late into the night. The interactive capabilities were getting there. The voice was perfect, but the cadence was just a little off. The 3-D model (which didn't have any clothes yet… she'd had to made certain guesses, based on the accounts of his groupies, old ladies, and two ex-wives) was a marvel. Alberta felt almost as though she could reach out and really touch Russell Aquarius.

So when she rolled over in bed the next morning, and actually *did* touch Russell Aquarius, her reaction was not quite what she would have expected.

She screamed like a little bitch.

Russell didn't respond. Didn't move. All he did was give a half-snore, and turn over.

He was nude, just like his avatar. Well, not quite: he did have a well-worn leather vest on. Barely covered by the sheet, she noted he was hairier than she thought he'd be. He stank of B.O. and patchouli oil. But… he was absolutely gorgeous. Every bit, and more, than she would have dreamed.

Inching away to get a better look, Alberta decided that must be it. She was dreaming. It *had* been an awfully late night.

Russell turned again, facing her. As if magnetically attracted to the female form, he groped across the bed until his hand met her thigh. "There's my girl..." he sighed, still snoozing.

Alberta's heart raced. His touch certainly felt real. His flesh was warm. There were even hardened calluses on his guitar-playing fingers.

Side 2, Track 1: *I Hate Sundays*

Russell woke to the malignant death rays of daylight. He hated mornings, always had, even well before his ascent from folk clubs to Filmores East and West and all the psychedelic blues joints he'd played in between. In fact, unless he was puking up peyote in the desert while hallucinating coyote gods, he pretty much didn't like daytime at all.

Worse than the piercing sun in his eyes was his bursting bladder. He had to piss like a Budweiser Clydesdale. He had to find the toilet, or at least a sink, right NOW. Even a trashcan would do, or an empty boot. He opened his eyes to a beady little squint and scanned the area for a place to relieve himself. He bravely lifted his head – for his brain was still spinning from the vodka and mescaline cocktails he imbibed the night before – and caught a glimpse of his bedmate.

Years ago he might have freaked to wake up in some unknown place and next to a naked stranger, having little or no memory as to how he got there, but this was now a regular occurrence. Almost a morning ritual for Russell. Maybe he had changed ever since he dropped all his girlfriends, or perhaps it was just the new scene now to spread the love (and the sex and the clap) to every new city he played. Oh well, he'd just go with the flow. And right now he had a flow of his own to take care of.

He gingerly lifted the covers and got out of bed – careful not to wake whoever the fuck he had been sleeping with and, naked save for the leather vest he always wore, headed for the door to the john.

He opened the door to find a walk-in clothes closet instead. Well, that would do if maybe he could find a cowboy boot or two to drain his dragon. He took a step inside and just as he did, he heard –

"Shit, shit, shit!" The girl suddenly screamed out from the bed and started throwing things all over the place. She must be having a bad trip, she was so out-of-control.

Without even a thought (it was *way* too early for coherent thinking) Russell instinctively dove into a pile of clothes at the back of the closet.

He could still hear the chick out there having some tantrum, yelling about her goddam alarm clock, how it didn't go off, how her phone didn't go off either and now – *Fuck! Fuck! Fuck!* – she was late again! Through a crack in the closet door he saw her hurl some kind of space age looking radio right at the closet. It sounded like it had broken into millions of pieces.

In the past, if he saw a groupie become unglued, he'd have hugged her, given her his famous smile, and helped her through her bad trip. But after that crazy chick who'd been stalking him in Dallas had come on the scene, he was fearful. It wasn't all just peace and love, grass and microdots, these days. Now there were groupies who were high on angel dust and wanted nothing better than to carve a swastika into your forehead, Manson Family-style, while you slept.

Through the door crack he caught only a glimpse of the girl, who was now feverishly searching around the place, picking up various articles of clothing and putting them on. They all looked the same after a while – brunettes, with long and perfectly straight hair, just the way he liked them. But, oh, how he prayed that this wasn't Crazy Dallas Chick.

Through the fog of drugs and alcohol, he tried to remember this girl he must've balled last night. But he couldn't evoke anything about her – her face, her name, where he'd even met her. He did have a few vague recollections of being with her in bed last night; feeling the contours of her body, how she had her eyes closed – like she was tripping on Blue Cheer – the whole time they were doing it. That was hardly disconcerting; it was a pleasant change from all the groupies who'd give off weird vibes staring at him the whole time with that *I-can't-believe-I'm-screwing-a-rock-and-roll star* look. And he remembered that the chick from last night's hair smelled good, like strawberries – and devoid of that Agent Orange'y smell of caked on hairspray most of his other groupies reeked of.

"Hi, it's me," he heard this girl saying, "It's Alberta. Yes, I *know* I'm late – it's my stupid alarm clock." She must be on the phone. He peered through the door crack. He could see her sitting at the foot of the bed. He couldn't see the phone receiver; she had some little communication device up to her ear, like something from *Star Trek*.

"OK," she said, "That's why I'm running out the door. Tell everyone I'll be in the office in 10 minutes."

Russell saw her jump off the bed and heard a door slam.

When he was certain that the girl was gone he exited the closet and found the bathroom, where he emptied a couple gallons of psychedelic-looking urine.

Stepping back into the bedroom he looked around. It wasn't the same pad he'd been in with Crazy Dallas Chick – CDC had no furniture – it was just a loft filled with dozens of rotted castaway doors, mostly Victorian, all stacked like sculptures throughout the place.

So maybe the girl he just saw was not Crazy Dallas Chick, after all. Of course, this could be CDC's *new* pad, but it looked a too little normal for that freak – this place at least had furniture: a night table, a desk and chair, and, of course, a bed. But then there were a bunch of weird machines, electric, no, maybe even *electronic* stuff. They reminded Russell of some of the trippy futuristic blinking contraptions he'd seen in Kubrick's *A Clockwork Orange*, only this stuff was smaller and less angular.

The place was interesting, but right now, Russell was more interested in sleep. He still didn't know where he was – he couldn't even remember what city he was in – but he was too tired and still buzzed from last night to care. Anyway, if someone needed him, his road manager Sid would find him. The dude always did.

For a brief moment, Russell worried about what might happen if and when this new psycho chick came back from her office, or wherever he overheard her say she was going. He thought about that uptight scene just moments ago, when she threw shit all over the wall, but that thought just came and went, like the chattering monkeys in his meditations. Even the memory of the feel of her body last night blurred to nothingness as Russell went from comfortably numb to even more comfortably zonked out.

Side 1, Track 2: *Smells Like My Spirit*

As Alberta drove home from the office – narrowly missing death's tap on the shoulder several times as she changed lanes on the 405 freeway in her fiesta-green Smart car – she replayed the morning over and over. And over again. She'd never had such a vivid dream.

She could have sworn she'd woken up, nude, next to the (long-dead) man she'd been obsessed with since puberty hit her like a two-by-four, but of course that was not possible.

While all her classmates were listening to Jesse McCartney and the Jonas Brothers through cheap ear-buds, Alberta had found true depth and meaning in the scratchy vinyl sermons of Russell Aquarius. (His given name was Russ Goldstein, but Alberta didn't like to think of him that way. He may have been born like any other mortal, but he lived like a god.)

When her Uncle Pete died, he'd bequeathed his entire vinyl record collection and his true vintage Linn Sondek LP12 turntable to 13-year-old Alberta. Why her? Alberta had never shown any interest in music before, and certainly not the hoary old bands

Pete dug – The Electric Prunes, The Box Tops, Strawberry Alarm Clock, Big Brother and the Holding Company. Russell Aquarius.

But when she was a little girl, too young to be able to read the names of the bands and laugh at them, Alberta had loved looking at the album covers. They were like primitive puzzles, with all their pieces and parts. Uncle Pete told her all about their origins – the fact that Andy Warhol collaborated with designer Craig Braun on the working zipper fly on the Rolling Stones *Sticky Fingers* LP (Alberta's mom didn't appreciate her playing with that one), and that a swanky London design firm called Hipgnosis had designed Led Zeppelin's *Houses of the Holy* gatefold of naked rock-climbing kiddies (another non-fave of Alberta's mom) as well as Pink Floyd's seminal *Dark Side of the Moon*. Through Uncle Pete, Alberta learned that Drew Struzan painted the Alice Cooper *Welcome to my Nightmare* album art.

And speaking of nightmares…

It was just information overload, she convinced herself, instinctively flinching as she stared up the undercarriage of the ever-braking, gigantic black Yukon in front of her. Last night she had processed more information on Russell than she'd ever seen all at once, and that was a lot. All those words, pictures, and videos.

She smiled. That avatar was damn good, though. So lifelike.

Which totally explained the realness of the dream. She could have sworn she felt the warmth of his hand on her thigh, though. And smelled his stringent manliness. She shook her head. Obviously, she was over-tired. Because after she'd fainted – or more likely, merely fallen back to sleep – she woke up alone in the bed. And late to the morning meeting. Not good. It was becoming a pattern, and she'd been warned. At least she'd saved the day with some kickass coding suggestions for the newest software.

Exiting onto Victory Boulevard, Alberta made a Mickey D's stop, and was soon home with her rather dismal dinner of chicken nuggets and limp fries.

The moment she unlocked her front door and stepped inside her modest apartment, she knew she hadn't been dreaming. The hairs rose on the back of her neck, and her heart pounded the way one's does when there's imminent danger… or the promise of sex. She felt that, too. A flush rose to her cheeks, and a pulse quickened in the V of her crotch. She stopped and stood still, her senses heightening. There it was. The smell of male sweat mingled with the earthy musk of sage, lavender, mint and marijuana.

Then she heard him singing. "Get in my Econoline van, I'll show you paradise wo-man…"

The small foyer was dim, and shadow-cast. The only light was ambient, coming from the glow of the screen of her laptop.

"Whew," she sighed audibly.

It was just the Russell avatar. She'd forgotten to turn the laptop off.

Flicking the overhead light on, she stepped into the living room and made her way to the pocket-sized computer nook and shut the lid.

She continued into the kitchen, where she set the bag of fast food down on the counter and kicked off her shoes. She put her purse and her briefcase on the butcher block, and reached for the nearest cupboard.

She opened it, took out a plate, and got some silverware. Just because she was eating junk didn't mean she had to dine like a barbarian.

She turned around, and – *smack!* Found herself thrust face-first in Russell Aquarius's narrow, furry chest. He was wearing her leopard robe from Victoria's Secret – the one with the black marabou trim – a bemused smile, and nothing else.

"Hey, babe," he said. "What's for dinner?"

Side 2, Track 2: *I Didn't Mean to Turn You Off*

The girl frowned at him. "What?! I thought I just turned you *off.*"

What a funny chick. "No, you blew my mind last night, dearie." He looked down the crack in his robe to see his member semi-erect. "And it looks like you're turning me on now." He'd been in these situations before – a lot of chicks lacked confidence in themselves and would start crying, thinking it was their fault if he couldn't fly his flag. But, with a little flattery and a pep talk, he could get the girls' heads on straight again. A little cocaine often helped, too.

"No, that's not what I'm talking about," said the girl. "I meant your avatar. I'm pretty sure I just turned you off."

"My what? My abattoir?" This chick's mind was somewhere out in Ruby Tuesday-land. He didn't know what in God's name she was talking about – she probably didn't, either – but that's cool, he'd play along. "You're a space cadet, but you're really a good egg," he said, giving her a hug while pushing his penis against her blouse. She smiled and gave him a lustful look. "That's my girl…" He patted her butt.

She was warming up to him, so he asked her again, "What's for dinner?"

"Well, I'm having Mickey D's, unless *you* made something for both of us."

He laughed. Everyone knew that Russell Aquarius didn't cook. Or clean. Or shave himself or even bathe himself. That's what groupies were for. He didn't bust his butt, giving fans the shows of their lives, expanding New Thought consciousness throughout the world while fighting for social justice, just to come home to do bourgeois domestic shit.

She showed him her fast-food dinner – those sorry-ass chicken shrivels. There were only nine pieces; she started to put half (4.5 of a "finger") on an extra plate for Russell, but he just grabbed a handful – at least six of them – and scarfed them down his throat before she could say anything.

"Oh thanks," she sighed, rolling her eyes. "Now what am I gonna eat?"

"You can have whatever's left," he said, licking his lips. "Anyway, I don't know which McDonald's you go to, but this swill tastes like a rat's ass, so you're better off not eating it. Plus, you could stand losing a few pounds –"

"What are you saying?" OK, she knew she wasn't skinny, but she had a better figure than just about anyone she worked with, except for that H-1 visa Uzbekistan bitch who thought she was hot shit and the best programmer in the company. At least Russell was actually skinny himself – she hated those bloated brogrammers with their pot bellies and double chins who wore shirts saying "No Fat Chicks." Also, she had recently watched Russell's concert footage from his last tour and, after seeing the audience, she remembered thinking how it was true after all: Americans really *had* gotten fatter in the past half-century.

"Come now, dearie. I wasn't saying you're obese or anything. In fact, *damn girl!* your body felt pretty *fucking* good last night." That seemed to placate her, for she smiled at him again.

She told him that she was hungry – they both were – so she made a fry-up from an eclectic mix of leftovers in the fridge. She poured two glasses of wine and sat them both down at the kitchenette to eat. He wolfed his food as if he hadn't eaten for 50 years and said little, other than the occasional "Mmm, good" and belching sounds.

She was picking at her food. "You're probably wondering my name."

He wasn't, but he said that she could tell him if it would make her feel more relaxed for what they were going to be doing after din-din. She looked confused, until he added that they'd be "flying united" tonight. To make his meaning a little more clear, he did the old in-out-in-out sign with his fingers. She blushed. Chicks like her were funny that way; they'd act all shy, but they both knew that they'd be balling within the hour.

She told him that her name was Alberta. To Russell, that was a pretty normal name. He was used to groupies with names like Sky, Daffodil, Rainbow, Mary Juana, and Luci in the Sky.

Alberta started to tell him a little about herself but he didn't seem too interested. Or maybe he didn't understand her contemporary jargon.

When the last of their ersatz dinner was chowed down, he gave her his plate. She obviously wasn't clear as to what that meant.

So he explained, "I'm giving you this so you can wash it or put it away, or whatever it is girls do to clean up."

He laughed at her and drank some more wine, this time straight out of the bottle. She looked at him with disgust and even made a theatrical sigh. Nevertheless, she picked up their plates and utensils and washed them in the sink.

"When you're done, lover," he said, walking to the bed, "I'll be right here. Impatiently waiting." He let the Victoria's Secret gown drop to the floor and got between the covers.

It was her turn to laugh. "Hmmm... You do have a cute little butt."

"That's my girl," he said.

The dishes could wait, but not her libido. She dropped trou and jumped on top of her rock and roll hero and avatar.

They started with a little tongue action and before long Russell had worked himself down her breasts. She suddenly pushed him away. "Uh...I'm sorry Russell, but I was running late this morning and had no time to shower."

"So?"

"Well, I don't want to gross you out or anything, but I probably reek."

"It's the 70s, for fuck sake," he said, kissing her breasts some more before slowly working his way south. "We're all children of the earth." He spread her legs. "Anyway, my sweet, sexy Albania –"

"Alberta."

"Whatever. As I was saying, you smell better than half of the chicks I balled this tour." That wasn't much of a come on, but it worked. She took his member and slid it inside her. Within minutes, he climaxed. Russell hit the pillow and started snoring immediately.

Side 1, Track 3: *Purple Craze*

Alberta tossed and turned for a few minutes, still marveling at the miracle snoring beside her. Russell Aquarius in *her* bed! Unthinkable. Not possible. But *soooo good.* She sighed and sat up, swinging her legs over the side of the bed. She sat for a moment, relishing the experience. Even (almost) loving his scent on her skin.

But she had to take a shower.

She padded into the adjacent room, and turned the faucet on. The water was hot immediately, and she stepped into its wet, warm embrace.

As Alberta went through the motions of washing and rinsing, her mind raced. Even though she'd been thinking about it all day, Russell's appearance had still been in the abstract. After all, she'd more than half-convinced herself she imagined the whole thing.

But now? Not now, as she still felt the aftershocks of him inside her.

He actually wasn't a very good lay. That was surprising, given his considerable experience in the sack. Then again, he was dead. She had to cut him a little slack on that account. Alberta shuddered... did this escapade make her a necrophiliac? "Ughhh."

Then her mind snapped to another, far more sobering possibility. What if she'd been knocked up? How would she explain *that* to her family?

Alberta's musings were interrupted by the shower curtain being pulled back, and Russell stepping inside to join her. *Whew*, she thought with relief. *He really needed a wash.*

"Hello, darlin'," he leered. "Be a doll and scrub my back, would you?"

After their shower, during which he hogged all the hot water, Alberta rustled up a pair of her yoga pants and a Rolling Stones 2015 *Zip Code Tour* tee-shirt for Russell. He was used to wearing women's clothing onstage, so bumming around her apartment in her finery was hardly a hair-turner for him.

Once he was dried and dressed, he started pacing around in her bedroom. "You holding?" he asked tightly.

Alberta, wrapped in a towel, raised her eyebrows. "Huh?"

"I'm jonesing, man."

"Ah. Yes. Of course." Alberta sat on her bed and opened the nightstand drawer. "I've got some medical marijuana here."

Russell cocked his head. "Medical?"

"Yeah. It's legal now. Just about anyone can get a prescription. Even my grandma has one." Alberta offered up the plastic bottle, full of bud. She held it aloft. "Girl Scout Cookies. The best."

"Groovy. Give it here."

She popped the top and extracted an already-rolled toothpick joint, and passed him a lighter.

He snatched them from her, lit up, and took a long draw. He took another, not offering her any.

"Ahhhhhh. Better." He paused. "Damn, girl. This is some good shit."

"As I said, it's pharmaceutical."

He grinned. "It ain't no skunk weed." He waited a beat, and then asked, "What else you got in that little goodie drawer of yours? Shrooms, acid, ups, downs, reds, black beauties, bennies, big chief, blow?"

Alberta shook her head. "But I've got Twinkies in the kitchen."

Russell was halfway out the door and down the hall in a flash. "Outta sight!"

Alberta, reclaiming her Victoria's Secret leopard robe with its black marabou trim, trotted out after him.

He'd already torn apart half the kitchen looking for the Twinkies by the time she caught up with him. They were on top of the fridge. "Here you go," she said, handing him a twin pack of sugar, sorbic acid 60, Red 40, mono and diglycerides, and calcium sulfate.

As he stuffed his handsome face, and looked at her with those deep, soulful blue eyes of his, Alberta broached the subject.

The. Subject.

"Russell," she began. "You said earlier, 'it's the 70s.' You know you died in 1971, right?"

He looked at her, chewing thoughtfully. He swallowed. "We never really die, man. Stardust can't expire."

"You don't understand. You were electrocuted onstage when you were 27 years old. I'm 30 now, but I wasn't born until 1986. Fifteen years *after* you passed away."

"Whoa. Mind-blowing." He stuffed half of the second Twinkie into his mouth. "Maybe, like these delicious desserts here, I'm just very well-preserved."

"Uhhhh. No. There was a funeral, and everything."

He raised his bushy blonde brows. "Hm." He thought for a moment. "Who came to my funeral? Was Plant there? I swear, that bastard stole my lyrics…" He shook his head. Gave her a long, hard look. "Nope. I don't believe you, Albatross."

"Alberta."

"Whatever."

She crossed her arms. "Look down."

He appraised the bulge in front of the yoga pants, and gave her a wolfish grin.

She shook her head. "At the shirt you're wearing."

Russell did so, bloodshot eyes peering at the text and squinting at the famous tongue-and-lips logo. His face went white. "Whoa. The Stones are *still* touring?!" He shook his head. "OK, now I know you're putting me on."

Alberta sighed. She got her smart phone out the pocket of her robe. She punched at the screen as Russell looked on quizzically. She held it up close to his face. "Check it out. *Behind the Music* on YouTube. The Russell Aquarius episode. It starts with footage from your last concert. Look."

Side 2, Track 3: *The Guest in the Machine*

Except for the few times when Russell jumped up, pointed an accusing finger at the funny-looking phone and yelled, "I never said that!" And later, "The lying, scum-sucking bastard!" he was strangely quiet throughout the entire 'Aquarius Rises and Falls' segment.

When it was over, he could feel the girl staring right at him. And she looked like she about to cry. "I'm sorry, Russell. I just thought you needed to know what happened to you."

The clip was only 15 minutes long, but to Russell it might have lasted years, even lifetimes. Everything was so heavy, so profound. He wanted to say something to make sense of what he'd just seen, or at least to cheer up this strange groupie with the weird name (Albany? Albania? Why couldn't he remember?) but no words would form in his brain.

Finally, he asked, "Babe, maybe I'm just one toke over the line but are you sure this is just grass? What else is in this shit?"

"Nothing. I told you, it's medicinal cannabis." She smiled at him.

The chick must be some sort of sorceress or priestess, or both. He took another look at that blinking phone gadget in her hand and then leaned back and closed his eyes. "I think... I'm... having... a bad trip."

"I'm sorry, Russell, I didn't bring your avatar to life to freak you out. I just programmed you because, well, I've been into you ever since I was a little girl. I'm fairly new to artificial intelligence so I may have screwed up by accidentally designing you with a consciousness of self. Maybe I can make some adjustments to your algorhythms –"

He waved her away. "No, no, whoever you are, please! Just stop talking this freaky talk. It's like I'm bumming on the brown tabs at Altamont." He looked like he was going to crash but suddenly grabbed the girl's bottle ("Evian" they called this water from the future) and splashed himself in the face with it the fluid. That snapped him to attention.

"Wait – before I peak," he told her, "I'm gonna enjoy this ride. Man, I could write a dozen albums about this mindfuck going on in my head right now. You know what? Be a love and go get me a pen and some paper, OK?"

The girl came back, muttering something about her having trouble finding a pen because nowadays everyone uses computers. That seemed pretty stupid to him – if this new age was so advanced, why didn't they just use mind power? Fortunately, the strange young woman presented him with some unlined paper and a red pen.

"Now, what were you saying, babe?" Russell looked at the girl like he was ready to take dictation. "Something about our lives being part of one huge – what did you call it, an avatar? – and we're all programmed inside it." He started writing.

"Well, that's not exactly what I said."

"Hold that thought, girl, I'm in my own head right now. Whoa! You wouldn't believe the vision I just had. I saw myself being born and I saw my life acted out in front of me – don't laugh – right in the palm of your hand. I even saw my own death. Or, I guess, how will die if I don't expand my consciousness and get rid of all those ego trips and all the head games people play. It's like one of those fucking cautionary tales, you know?" He scribbled some more. "It's clear as a bell that if I don't get my shit together the heavens will rain down upon me and smite me with a thunderbolt." He drew a little diagram with pictogram Russell being zapped by Thor.

"Actually, Russell, and I don't mean to be so morbid, what killed you was electrocution from the mic."

"Oh, that's a good metaphor." He wrote that down too. Then, for several hours, he scribbled page after page while the potent drug coursed through his veins. He only stopped when the girl – the witch who could hold people's futures in her palms – said that that she had no more "printer" paper. He wrote "PRINTER PAPER" on the margin of his last page, convinced that later, when he was indeed straighter, these two words would add some significance to all these hallucinations.

When he'd not only used up all the printer paper but also had written on all the margins – and then wrote more on some toilet tissue, he lay back, exhausted, completely spent physically and creatively.

Suddenly, without warning, Russell went into a fetal position and cried.

The girl who held the future came over and wrapped her arms around him. "What's wrong?" she asked.

"I just saw life! LIFE! With no illusions; the whole enchilada of cosmic consciousness. From alpha to omega." He wiped the tears from his eyes. "There are no words to describe this, it's like I was born and reborn in the blink of an eye. But it's too much, too fucking beautiful, man, the whole mindfuck, amigo. But now my mind is gone – for good! Fuckin' A, I'm gonna be a headcase casualty like Syd Barrett." He cried again. "Don't you see, woman? Knowing what I now know, I can never go back to this illusion we call the real world. And there's no way I'm gonna ever go back on stage, only to be killed by heaven's wrath!"

She stroked his hair. "You don't need to worry about that, hon. 'Hon'? I don't know why I even called you that. I'm not your girlfriend... right? Anyway, everything's going to be OK. You can never go back onstage or live in what you call the real world again. *You're* not even real."

He shot her a look. "Is that supposed to make me feel better?"

"I guess I shouldn't talk to you like that. Sorry."

"If you're some angel or spirit that was sent from the future, you have the worst bedside manner."

"You're right. Listen, you go get some sleep. In the morning you can look at your notes and work the Russell Aquarius magic on them."

"Thanks, foxy. I already got an idea for a song cycle."

"Then you just sleep it off, my genius, and tomorrow you can get started."

"But I'm gonna need a guitar. Or piano, or something."

"I'll find you whatever you need. You just get some sleep." She grabbed a blanket from her bed and covered him up. "In the meantime," she added, mostly to herself, "I'll see if I can find some tweaks to reprogram you."

"I told you, no more freaky talk." He weakly waved her off, pulled the blanket over his head, and started snoring.

Side 1, Track 4: *Sunshine Stupor, Man*

As Russell slumbered, Alberta worked late into the night on his avatar. But there was nothing wrong with it, that she could find. The code was perfect, and everything was configured as it should be. Even the wonky speech pattern had self-corrected. But there was something very strange about it. She couldn't quite figure it out. She half-considered taking the laptop to work in the morning to see if that skinny Uzbek bitch Guldasta could help her figure it out.

But what if Russell got deleted somehow? Alberta wasn't sure whether or not the avatar was like some kind of virtual voodoo doll… she wouldn't take that chance.

Even though Russell was kind of a jerk, and a slob, Alberta couldn't help but feel protective of him. She had to remind herself that times were different when Russell was around, and even though his lyrics made it seem he truly loved and revered women, the reality was probably a lot different.

She could change him.

Before she knew it, it was nearly dawn and she hadn't slept a wink. Alberta made a pot of coffee, poured herself a mugful, and entered a to-do list into her phone. Number 1 was a guitar for Russell. There was a Guitar Center on Ventura Boulevard she could hit after work, then she'd stop and get him some new clothes. She figured eventually he'd have to go out in the world. (A fantasy played out in her mind, of her introducing Russell to her parents as her new boyfriend.) Another thing she needed to do was go to the grocery store – Russell was eating her out of house and home already. She thought about putting condoms on the list, but figured whatever damage to be done had been done. Thank goodness herpes and AIDS hadn't been a part of Russell's era.

After she perked up a bit thanks to the caffeine and sugar, Alberta went into the bedroom and got dressed. At least she wouldn't be late this morning. She stood for a moment, pausing in the doorway between her room and the hallway, marveling at Russell's prone form. He'd called her a witch. Maybe she was; how else could such strange magic be explained?

Suddenly, he stirred and his eyes half-opened. He smiled at her, all charm.

"Where are you going, Albacore?"

"Alberta."

"Whatever."

"I'm going to work."

"Cute. You told me what you do, but like… What do you do?" He sat up. "I'll bet you're a secretary."

"No. I'm an Augmented Reality Systems Analyst and Programming Head."

"Head? You could've fooled me." He winked. "You know, it wouldn't hurt you to get kinky once in a while…"

Alberta knew she had her work cut out for her, but now was not the time. Not when she was *on time*, for once. "Look. I've gotta get to the office. There's fresh coffee in the kitchen, and I'm going to the store tonight. Any special requests?"

"You mean aside from…?" He paused. What kinds of foods might they have in this brave new world ruled by Ken Kesey and the Merry Pranksters, and seemingly ripped from the pages of *Slaughterhouse Five*? Freeze dried astronaut packets, shriveled chicken "nugget" things, leftovers and Twinkies was about it, judging from this chick's previous offerings.

"Yes. Aside from *that*. How about pizza?"

Russell nodded. "Yeah, babe. Pizza would be great." He got up, and walked over to her.

Alberta tensed when Russell hugged her. She wasn't sure why, but something (well, *everything*) seemed odd. Even though he'd recently showered, he smelled strong again. The patchouli oil scent was overwhelming. It was like every new morning was still his first in the present-day.

"Lemme walk to you to the door, dearie," he said sweetly.

Alberta was slightly concerned one of the neighbors might catch a glimpse of the nude rock star. As she opened the front door and stepped out, Russell leaned forward to give her a kiss, and–

–His entire face fragmented and then all but *disappeared!*

Russell staggered back inside, clutching his head. He swayed, but was instantly back to normal. His face was all together, and handsome as ever.

Alberta's eyes must have been the size and shape of saucers, because Russell regarded her with deep concern.

"What just happened?" he asked, his voice faint.

"You – you pixelated!" Alberta cried.

He shrugged, not knowing the word.

She fixed him with a hard, no-nonsense stare. "I have to go to work. But Russell, listen to me: Do not try to leave this apartment. It could kill you."

He laughed, his voice already back to full strength. "But haven't you been saying I'm already dead, babe?" He looked at her with a mixture of wonder and pity. "You are one far-out chick. Don't worry about me. I'm going back to bed."

Side 2, Track 4: *Whatever Gets You Thru the Light*

Russell was feeling OK after last night's intense trip *until* he got up and kissed the girl goodbye. As soon as she opened the door to go, Russell suddenly felt light-headed, like he was fading out – literally. The angry sun zapped photons through his eyes and right through his skull. It was like everything around him had been bleached itself into nothingness. This must be a flashback from last night, he thought. But this was even more intense than the flashbacks he'd had for weeks after going in a cave in Laguna with Leary and hitting nine tabs of windowpane.

Russell threw himself back into bed and burrowed under the covers. Then he tossed and turned. He didn't feel so queasy once he got back in bed. And his thoughts raced, thinking about that long, strange trip he took last night. He couldn't get the image of this far-out chick in this far-out pad here out of his head. Especially that hallucination of her holding that glowing device – the gizmo from the future which recorded his whole life and death. Not only was last night the trippiest of his life, but the more he thought about it, this whole time with this Dilberta chick, or whatever her name was, was trippy. Like one of Poe's opium fantasies.

How long had Russell been here? A couple nights? Weeks? It didn't matter, he was hip on sticking around for a while. He'd trusted his intuition, gone with the flow his whole life and that had brought him close to fame and fortune. He had gained a world stage where he could both boogie and radiate a higher consciousness, scoring with hundreds of women – single, married, lesbian, even, and acquired some bitchin' cars along the way. His instincts now were to do some writing around this chick's pad for a few days. This strange place was inspiring. Plus, he didn't feel like going out – he'd just been flown in from playing some festival at the Isle of Lucy – and he needed to mellow.

He scratched his greasy head. *Wait! Did we even play that gig?* He couldn't remember anything about the Isle of Lucy other than the pouring rain and mud.

Russell got out of bed and drank some more coffee. He had vague memories of taking notes during last night's trip. But where were they? He looked around – on the nightstand, on the desk, on the kitchenette table – but with no success.

Then he looked under the bed. *Eureka!* There was a stack of paper filled with observations, drawings, lyrics, chord changes, obscene doodles, and the occasional rantings of a lunatic. The first page had tear-shaped watermarks. He recalled crying last night, though he couldn't remember why. The last few pages were stuck together with dried semen. He didn't remember letting it all hang out last night, but it wouldn't have surprised him if he had.

He eagerly went through the stack of notes, underlining sentence after sentence. To Russell, this stuff was hipper than Dylan's. Russell, of course, idolized the Bard of Fourth Street, but that was the

60s and this is the 70s, man. Russell resolved to write something big, bigger than any Wagnerian *Gesamptkunstwerk.* Bigger than anything Townsend could ever dream up.

And Russell had always been a huge fan of Arthur C. Clarke, Asimov, Heinlein, all those sci-fi cats. Russell's father was a physicist, and though Russell and the old coot had little else in common, they both were fascinated with astronomy. Irving was more interested in the scientific aspects – measuring and naming the universe. Russell's fascination with the cosmos was in its limitlessness, with all its philosophical and mind-blowing implications. And his interest in space was years before he'd blown his mind on various consciousness-expanding drugs. And *before* last night, when his mind melded into a different dimension from that chick's far-out grass laced with holy-fuck-knows-what.

Russell circled a few key phrases. Deep stuff about how he was programmed after he died, like a robot or something, and that he had been designed to have no sense of self, but through some error (by the gods, maybe?) he was now developing an ever-higher consciousness. How he needed to lose his ego and how he had attained a newly enlightened state by getting zapped by Zeus's thunderbolt. And how all the atoms in his body must now be stored into a tiny, but powerful computer. And how the girl told him he was an avatar. He remembered, from his time in India, that an avatar had been described to him as some kind of divine teacher whose soul was supposed to exist beyond the physical world. So he was cool being an avatar.

Russell's thoughts turned to an unpleasant dinner he'd had with his parents when he'd just flown in from Bombay in '68. His dad's eyes rolled every time that Russell had mentioned his personal swami. The dinner went from bad to worse when he started talking to the old man about astrology. "Studying the universe," Irving had told him, "*that* I can understand. But predicting the future through arbitrary and superstitious astrological signs?! That's crazy, like the Zodiac Killer."

Irving was old, but to Russell, his dad was no old soul. Russell wondered if his father, or even his mother – dear Myrna – would ever achieve the state of consciousness that he had attained in the relatively short time he'd been on this planet. But then, what could you expect? Mom was a Gemini and Dad was a Cancer. Everyone knows that's trouble.

That reminded him that he should call Gunta, his astrologer. He could find out from her whether the stars were opportune to begin writing this new cosmic rock opera.

But where did that girl with the Canadian name (Vancouver? Saskatchewan?) leave her little telephone robot?   It seemed to him like she carried it everywhere. But there it was, right on the desk.

Russell looked at the crazy gadget and tried to figure out how to make the phone call. He'd dialed Gunta's number so many times at all hours of the day and night for a zodiac reading that fortunately, he knew he number by heart. But there were no dials, no switches. The thing could've come from the year 2525 for all he knew, like some obelisk to apes built by sophisticated aliens. He tried to remember how the girl tapped on the thing to make a phone call. Then he pointed, punched, and jabbed all around the phone.

He hit some buttons and a weird dial tone, then some ringing, and suddenly he heard a voice. He put the phone up to his ear.

"Hello?" It was a male voice. "Alberta? Are you there, or did you just butt-dial me?"

Side 1, Track 5: *Sweet Home Alberta*

As soon as she got home from work (loaded down with a second-hand acoustic guitar, its accessories, clothes for him, and fast food for them), Alberta saw that Russell had once again made a complete shambles of her apartment. She was already pissed she'd left her phone at home and was without Instagram all day long, so this was the cherry on top of the crap cake. She set the bounty down on the floor just inside the door and took a disapproving look around, taking stock of the mess.

The mayonnaise jar was left open on the kitchen counter, surrounded by crumbs. There was a mostly-gnawed crust lying on the floor. The dishes weren't washed.

In the living room, his crumpled papers were all over the place. He'd left an ink pen stain on her white ottoman.

She stepped into the bathroom. He'd not only left the toilet seat up again, but his aim hadn't improved one whit. Limp strands of his hair lay in the sink like wet Daddy Long Legs spiders.

And there he was, snoring away in her bed, the $200 satin bedspread kicked to a wrinkled mass at his feet.

Alberta started dreaming up the many ways in which she could do away with her rude rock star roomie.

Maybe, Alberta thought, she could get rid of Russell with some tried-and-true musicians' bane. Draw him a nice warm bath, add a little heroin and the *Collected Works of Aldous Huxley*, then let him break on through to the other side. Make him a big, juicy ham sandwich. Suggest The Hell's Angels act as his private security. Ply him with alcohol, then put him to bed resting on his back. Charter him a private plane, and pray for rain. Force him to read all his bad reviews, then leave him alone with a leather belt and bottle full of Reds. Or perhaps just simply electrocute him (it worked once... well, kind of).

Or better yet – she'd blow his mind with all the American events, pop culture and politics of the past 40-some years. The end of the Vietnam War. Peter Lemongello. The impeachment of Tricky Dick Nixon. Arena rock, disco, punk, hair metal, pop, grunge, DJ's, auto tune, YouTube. Traci Lords. 9/11. The Bush's in office. The extinction of the female bush. AIDS. OCD. GPS. Katrina. The first black president. Google glass. Reality TV and the advent of the Kardashian craze. Grumpy Cat. Or she could just play him the R.E.M. song *It's the End of the World As We Know It (And I Feel Fine)*. His blonde head would just explode. (*Kind of like it had that morning*, she thought with a shudder.)

What if she merely deleted the avatar she'd created? Would *that* do the dastardly deed?

Alberta sighed, sitting on the edge of the bed. She looked over at Russell, so innocent and boyish-looking as he slept.

No, she couldn't do any of those things. Alberta wasn't a killer, and besides – she felt responsible for Russell's current state of existence. It would be like aborting a 72-year-old baby.

She reached out and touched his bony shoulder. She gave him a gentle, rousing shake.

"Ungha, huh-wha-a-h?" He muttered. He turned onto his back and his eyelids fluttered. So did Alberta's heart. Even though he was a chauvinistic slob who screwed like he was plowing a dirt field, she was still a fan.

"Hey, babe," he said with a lazy smile.

"You still don't remember my name, do you?" she asked, also smiling in spite of herself. "I brought you some clothes, dinner, and –" at this last bit of news, he leapt from the bed as if spring-loaded – "a guitar."

The guitar was like a homing device. Russell knew exactly where to find it. Picking it up gently, reverently, by its neck, he marveled, "A '62 Gibson Hummingbird. Whoa. I smashed one of these onstage at the Avalon." He hugged the flaxen wood body to his chest, wrapping his arms around it. "I'm sorry," he muttered to the guitar.

"I have that concert on Blu-ray," Alberta said. "You were amazing." She swallowed, gathering her courage. "Would you please play *Acid Rain* for me...?"

His head dipped. "If you know as much about me as you say you do, my chubby little witch, then you know I don't play that song anymore."

"I'm sorry, hon," she sighed. "I shouldn't have asked."

Russell sat cross-legged on the floor, and began strumming. He made a few tuning adjustments, and tried a few more chords. He nodded, satisfied.

"I bought you some picks," Alberta said, reaching for the plastic bag. "Also, there's a modification kit here; it will allow you to plug the guitar into my laptop and use it as an amp. In fact, you can even upload melodies directly into iTunes as you write a song, make a playlist and store it in the cloud."

He looked at her blankly. "Um… OK."

Alberta thought about the questions she could ask Russell, now that he was here. She was always especially interested in his album covers. She never could find out who designed them.

Russell looked up. "Alpaca, is that food I smell? Man, I feel like I did that time I tripped out on Yellow Sunshine with my tour manager, holed up in Carey's Castle in Joshua Tree for 10 days in the summer of '66. I'm so hungry, I could eat the north end of a southbound billy-goat."

"Oh, yeah," Alberta nodded, reaching for the rest of the bags. As she took the food, and the clothes, into the kitchen.

Russell got up and followed her.

Alberta first handed him the jeans and western-style shirt she'd bought him. She took a guess on the waist size of the vintage dungarees, but knew it was smaller than hers – even so, they were loose on him. The shirt wasn't a Nudie – she couldn't afford that – but she'd gotten something close to what Russell (or Graham Nash) would have worn back in the day. Russell put the outfit on, and smiled at her.

"Food," he prompted. "And I hope it's not those chicken nuts again."

"Nuggets," Alberta replied. "And no. I got us some Chinese take-out."

As Russell dove in, using his chopsticks like a champ as she dug at her sticky rice with a plastic spork, Alberta asked if he liked the guitar.

"I love it, babe," he replied. "Thank you."

"That's the first time you've thanked me for anything," she said softly.

"I'll play you some of the songs I've been writing. I've been at it all day. Like the Mad Monk Grigori Rasputin, woman – I am unstoppable. You could shoot me, stab me, strangle and drown me, and I'd still be writing songs! I'm a machine, like that little robot you play with all the time." He swallowed a half-chewed mouthful of sweet-and-sour pork, gulping. "You left it here this morning, you know."

"My phone? Yeah, I know." She paused. "You didn't touch it, did you?"

"Of course I did. I've got a, what'ya call it, a curious nature."

Alberta stood. "Where is it?"

"Mellow out, woman. Your robot is fine."

She sat back down.

"OK."

"The sound quality is killer," Russell continued, still scarfing down chunky pork. "And no operator to connect long distance calls?" He shook his head. "Outta sight."

"You made a phone call?"

"I think so. The dude I talked said you call with your butt all the time." Russell chuckled. "How'ya do *that*, babe?"

"Who was it?"

Russell swallowed, then stretched. "He said you usually hang up on him." The rocker sighed, then closed his eyes. He oh-so-slowly searched his fried memory. "I'm thinking. Um... was it Eric? Derek? No..."

"Merrick? You talked to *Merrick*?"

Russell sat up straighter. "That's the one! Seemed surprised he was still on... uh, what'ya call it, speed dial. Since you two broke up and all."

Alberta dropped her spork. "You talked to my ex? What did you tell him?"

"I told him to leave you alone, because you're *my* old lady now. Once I get this double concept album done, you and me – we're going on the road." Russell picked up the white fold-together bucket of Chinese, put one corner to his lips, and dumped the remaining contents directly into his mouth. He swallowed, half-choking. "I'm gonna play a song I wrote for just for you, Albino."

Side 2, Track 5: *The Fawning in the Age of Aquarius*

He started the song with some filigreed guitar fingerpicking, in the English folk style of John Renbourn. Russell avoided eye contact with the girl as he began to sing, not out of uncertainty about the lyrics, but because he was kind of getting hung up about her. Still, he'd dug a lot of other chicks only to break their hearts, so he wanted to be careful not to let this tripped-out Albino girl get her hopes up.

In a smooth falsetto he sang:

She carries the sun
In the palm of her hand

The soul's priestess to consecrate
My soul's eternal plan.
Albino, you're my flash of white light
My furry freak angel
My future tonight
Albino
Let's take it slow
And let it flow
But just don't go,
Oh, Sweet White Albino...

Russell finished with a shimmery minor 9th chord that hung in the air. Then he finally looked to Alberta to see her reaction.

Through Alberta's cloud of tears, she too looked straight at him, or more like, straight *through* him. How many times since her angst-ridden tweens had she cranked up Russell's music and sat on her bed, just looking at the walls, wishing and hoping that life would get better?

"Hey, Albino! Earth to Albino!"

She finally refocused on his eyes.

"Whad'ya think, my lady? Damn good, right?"

"Yes and your voice has never sounded better!"

He patted her on the head. It wasn't uncommon for Russell to have people gush about his voice, especially women in intimate settings. He'd been critical of all the plate reverb that his old producers had insisted on, objecting that it destroyed the immediacy of his voice and took away from his lyrics.

"I tell ya, you've definitely been my muse, man. And this far-out pad has been my muse, too. I've decided I'm gonna crash here for a while, so I can get my head together." He looked her in the eye. "Where *we* can get head together."

"What do you mean 'we', white man? Er, Paiute man." She forgot for a second that he was 1/8 Native American. "Both of us will not be getting blow jobs."

"Sorry, babe, I guess I said 'we' 'cause, I don't know, you have two lips; plus, it's a team effort; you need a fellator and a fellatee." He laughed. "Except for this dude I saw in Amsterdam – a total solo act…"

Russell was already on the bed, fully clothed except for his exposed member and a look of incredulity.

She rolled her eyes. If she was going to change him, she knew she had to do it with tough love. "Then Russell, why don't you make like that self-interfering Dutchman and go suck yourself."

"Come on, Albion, you're not being constructive. I need you to release my sexual energy so that I can get some more writing done."

She ignored him. She started to type on her laptop, which had been sitting open on the nightstand.

I'll just go with the flow right now, he thought. The chick could let it all hang out later. Except for most of his groupies who'd climax while watching him onstage, some of the other girls were a little more uptight. Though this Albierto gal was usually horny all the time; maybe she needed a little more time tonight to get her lady rocks off.

He looked at all the gibberish she'd written on the computer and couldn't help giving her a little shit. "So what's so important that my lady can't orally pleasure her man now?"

"Well, if you must know, Russell, I'm researching how to program avatars for short term and long term storage, and how to save your learned memories."

"Oh, so you're trying to store me away?" He was still on the bed with his member out, but was completely flaccid and whenever he moved, the rock star's penis bobbed up and down like a useless or vestigial appendage.

"Well, I don't want to store you away for long. It's just that I can't have you around 24/7."

"24 *what?*"

"Never mind. I'm just saying that you can't be turned on all day and all night, making messes, and getting bored when I'm not around."

Russell looked dejected. Even his cock looked uncharacteristically sad. He tucked it away and zipped up, careful to avoid catching his pubic hairs.

"Russell, I think this is for your own good, too. All I need is a few hours, hon, and I can tweak your program so that you will be refreshed when you power up, and you will still remember all the times we have together. *And* remember all the great music you're writing."

Whatever she was saying was groovy with him. Russell still didn't know what the chick was talking about half the time, but more and more, he respected her intelligence and would give her the benefit of the doubt. She certainly was not one of those gals she herself would call "BASIC bitches." And of course in addition to her brains, she had nice ta-tas and a sweet ass.

This chick with the weird name (or names?) wasn't only becoming his lady, but more importantly, his muse. And some kind of oracle, too.

Can someone be both a muse and an oracle? He'd never thought about that before. He never had any reason to. Still, he was beginning to think he was falling for this chick, hard. He wanted to give her the good news.

"Ablucia."

She stopped typing.

"I want you to know that I've really been grooving on you." He leaned forward and delicately ran his fingers through her hair. "I want to get to know everything about you, I want to get inside your head and find out what makes you tick." She smiled. "And later I want to take your legs – which were just made to be spread – and screw you silly."

Alberta was flattered, of course. Although she had been meticulous in her research and in her coding to ensure that her avatar would speak, think, move, sing, and play guitar like the real Aquarius, she hadn't programmed him to be sexually attracted to her.

And she hadn't programmed him to be able to learn things and to have a consciousness, just like the real thing. Maybe even better – this A.I. simulacrum of Russell seemed far more introspective than the living Russell Aquarius.

Of course, to her this avatar was just as genuine as any person, far more real even than a dead icon. This Russell could certainly be a pain in the ass, and in desperate need of bathroom hygiene skills, but she liked him anyway. A lot more than that weasel, Merrick. She knew she needed to find a way to keep Russell's program handy on her desktop so she could call him up anytime she wanted good music, some laughs, and a 60s rock god shag.

He watched her start clicking a ball the girl claimed was a mouse, and studied the screen as alphanumeric codes dashed up and down. These programs and commands, she'd told him, functioned as his new brain and body.

As the reams of codes made their way down each computer page, Russell noticed that occasionally advertisements would pop up on the screen, like a Charlie Brown thought bubble. It pissed him off. Avatar or not, he was no sell-out like The Doors. In '66, they took 75 grand for a car ad. In that pathetic TV commercial, the band's hit *Light My Fire* was reduced to a fucking jingle, changing the lyrics from "Come on baby light my fire" to "Come on Buick light my fire."

That made him think about the parallel to his current situation. As much as he was digging his sweet little Prince-Albert-in-a-Can, he still wasn't crazy about chicks trying to change him. If he had a dime for every woman who tried to get him out of his bag and into hers, he'd have a second Bentley by now.

He tried to be as gentle as possible. "Stop it, please. I mean all this computer stuff."

She kept her fingers on the keyboard, but ceased typing and looked at him.

"You're wasting your time, Albuprion. You can't save me. No one can. And you can't change me, no matter how many robots and time machines you have."

"Russell, sweetheart, I'm not trying to change who you are," the girl looked him squarely in the eye. "And I'm not trying to save your soul. I am trying to save YOU, you as a corporeal being, you as a sentient being. Don't you see? I'm trying to save that brilliant man who is in the creative prime of his life – or the creative prime of his death, depending on how you look at it – from extinction. If I were to just shut you down right now, we would lose you forever."

"Couldn't you just buy another Russell Aquarius avatar?"

"I made this avatar from scratch. It's my code."

"Like... Morse code?"

"Not even close. There are programmers who make and sell rock star avatars, but they all suck." She made a couple clicks on the keyboard and some photos popped up. "I mean, look at this!" She showed him the laptop screen, "Some guy in New Jersey is selling his own Russell Aquarius avatar. And he's also got a Robert Plant avatar, by the way –"

"Say it's not so!" Russell wailed. "Not after Plantie stole my 'Ain't no Old Shep gonna happen again' line?" Russell was more upset at the mention of the Zeppelin front-man than he was at the thought of his own extinction.

He wasn't too worried about that: Though he wasn't able to reach his old astrologer, Gunta, after telling Merrick off, Russell did get someone else on the line. It was a boy named Julio. Julio told him that it was a bad day for Geminis. "When you mean 'bad'," Russell asked the fellow by way of explanation, you really mean 'good', like James Brown's *Superbad*, right?" And the guy said, 'Yeah, right." This new astrologer seemed like a solid freak. So nothing bad could happen to him today. Plus, the dude assured him that Russell's life would be good until Venus collides with Virgo at an IHOP.

But Russell was not going to be happy if that loser from Jersey kept selling those piss-poor Russell Aquarius avatar knockoffs. This dipshit's avatar moved around as if Russell were afflicted with Parkinson's, and the voice was much lower and menacing than his real voice. More like an avatard. Alberta told Russell that the Jersey fuck-head must have given it a Darth Vader voice, whatever that was. Worst of all, for Russell, was seeing his own faults caricatured in the avatar. It was the saddest impersonation of an arrogant, self-aggrandizing, and self-involved singer-slash-cunt since Sinatra.

"Fuckin'-A, Albahaca! This Jersey avatar makes me look like a megalomaniac, like some kind of Andrew Loog Oldham!"

"And you're not?" Alberta drolly asked.

"Well, OK, I used to be. But that was before you showed me that robot and I learned how I needed to break through the ego to find self-realization. And speaking of self-realization, I need a tape recorder, babe. I've got some trippy ideas I've got to record NOW before they disappear."

Side 1, Track 6: *The Song Remains the Game*

Alberta smiled at him. "Hon, I'm sorry to tell you this, but there are no tape recorders anymore. It's all digital now."

Russell blinked, not understanding. "But I can still record, yes?"

Alberta nodded. "Yep. You can even record directly into my phone, but I need to take it with me to work in the morning…"

"In the morning? But I need to record NOW, woman." He got off the bed and stomped one filthy bare foot on the floor. "NOW!"

"OK, OK," Alberta retorted snippily. "I have an old Sony handheld around here somewhere."

She got up started digging through the junk drawers in her living room and kitchen, Russell looking over her shoulder the whole time.

He nuzzled at her neck. "We could ball first."

She turned her head and kissed him full on the lips. Then went back to digging in the drawer. "Here it is!" she exclaimed, holding the tiny recording device aloft.

He took it between his thumb and forefinger and eyed it suspiciously. "How does this pipsqueak connect to a reel-to-reel?"

"It doesn't," Alberta replied. It records and plays back all by itself. Not as good as the computer, but I think that's a little advanced for you."

Russell looked hurt. "Babe, I can use an Electrodyne remix fully loaded console with a patch bay featuring a 24 input XLR microphone panel that directly feeds the mic preamps, and an ELCO panel with my hands tied behind my back."

It was Alberta's turn to look confused. She just sighed and said, "Well, with this all you have to do is press play and record at the same time."

He shrugged, and still carrying the guitar by its neck, sat on the sofa, tuned up, and began recording.

Alberta was half-enthralled, half-exhausted. "I'm going to bed," she announced, stifling a yawn. "I have to go to work extra early in the morning, so if I don't talk to you then – please don't touch my computer, or anything except the recorder and your guitar, until I get home."

Russell nodded absently, lost in his new riffs and melodies.

Side 2, Track 6: *Bandwidth on the Run*

As soon as Alberta walked in from work the next day she found Russell pecking away at the number keypad of her laptop. "NO!" She ran over and grabbed his hands off the keyboard. "Jesus H. Fuck, what were you doing?!" She was out of breath. "You scared me! Look, Russell, I care about you – you know that. I mean, beyond us hooking up, right?"

He looked at her blankly. Then he gave her a peace sign.

She continued. "But this is very important, Russell – to you, to your career, to us – don't mess around on the computer. One wrong stroke of the key and you would be fried – everything that is you, your soul, would be erased. Gone."

"Would it erase every record of my existence?" He seemed strangely unconcerned about that possibility. Just a couple days ago he would've had a tantrum if he thought that history would forget him.

"No. I mean, not unless the whole internet broke down, I guess."

"Now, my chubby little witch," he said, putting his arm around her. "Don't you worry your pretty head about it; I won't touch that computer from now on." He gave her a gentle kiss on the back on her neck. She was melting. "I need talk to Sid A-S-A-P. There's a line I wrote in this song that didn't end up making it on *Peace Mantra* and I need the exact lyric.

It's fucking perfect for something my new *Cosmic Tour* album."

"Even if Sid's still alive, what makes you think he'd still have your lyrics?"

"Sid would have them. He's a good guy. I gave him a mimeographed copy right before I left for the Isle of Lucy. I gave Sid Xeroxes of just about everything I worked on – it's 'cause…" He paused in mid-thought. "I'm sure you know about how that Crazy Dallas Chick burned up my garage?"

She shook her head. "I've studied you for years, read books, got a 10-year pin for my time on Russell Aquarius chat rooms, but I never heard anything about that."

"Well, Sid made sure he kept it under wraps. And made sure I never saw CDC again. Anyway, I would've called him on your robot if you had the courtesy to have left it with me."

"Sorry my dear, dead icon." Even Russell could detect that sarcasm. "But some of us are still alive and they have to work for a living, and part of that work is always being available by robot. That's how the world works nowadays. And, actually it's called a cellphone."

"Then give me the 'self-phone.' Please, my lady."

She gave it to him, after bringing up the keypad screen. Still, she doubted he'd get through. It was just dumb luck (*bad* dumb luck) he'd reached Merrick yesterday. That old number he had for Sid couldn't possibly still work and besides, even if the guy was still alive he'd probably be 90 years old by now.

Russell pressed the series of digits he said he knew by heart and it started ringing.

Alberta thought this could get embarrassing – she didn't like the idea of her Caller-ID going out there to some weirdo, so she took the phone back and put it on speaker.

"Hello." An elderly lady answered, her voice creaky.

"May I speak with Sid?"

"WHO?" she shouted, obviously half-deaf.

"Sid Greenblatt. This is his office, right?"

The woman gave a baritone gravel smoker's cough. Then she cackled.

Alberta was just about to hang up the phone when they heard, "Sidney? Somebody's calling for you. They think it's still your office." A final cackle was heard, which trailed into nothingness.

Another elderly (male, and not amused) voice came on. "This is Sid Greenblatt. Who's this?"

Russell grinned, and nodded at Alberta. "It's me, Siddy, I'm here shakin' my furry freak fur, looking for a lid of shrooms and some leg for tonight."

"…Who is this?"

"You know, baby, The Real Aquarius –"

Alberta could tell from the silence this call was going downhill fast. She didn't want the guy to hang up. "Mr. Greenblatt, my name is Alberta."

"Who?"

"Yeah, who?" Russell chimed in.

"I work in the field of artificial intelligence – and I also happen to be a life-long fan of Russell Aquarius's music. And, gosh, it's like I've read so much about you, to talk to a man who was the business brains behind the genius –"

"Hmph," the old man grunted. "Enough with the West Texas circle jerk. What do you want?"

"Well, sir, based on my computer knowledge and gleaning from thousands of accounts of Russell's life, I've made what – well, what you just heard – I've made what I think is the most realistic avatar ever. Definitely the only one that learns and has a true sense of its own being. So I really wanted to ask you to see him and tell me what you think." She paused. "How thoughtless of me, sir. An avatar is–"

"Yes, I fucking know what an avatar is. Do you Skype? Put him on it for me. Let me see this creation of yours."

With just a couple technical glitches, the three of them were soon face-to-face, as it were.

Then Sid and Russell (Russell 3.0, that is) eyed each other without saying a word. Well, in Sid's case, it was 'eye' – he had only one, while a black leather patch covered what must have been a hideous hole on the right side of his puckered face.

Finally Sid broke the silence by saying, "That is magnificent. He looks perfect. You did a great job."

Before Alberta had a chance to acknowledge the compliment, Russell said, "Thanks, man." Then he broke into song, "I'm lookin' alright, you're not looking too good yourself." Russell stopped singing and added, "Oh, and Siddy, baby, I need the lyrics to *Scorpio's Mantra*. Can you bring 'em over?"

Sid cracked up. "Alberta, I've got see this thing for myself."

How come this geezer can remember my name after five minutes but that prick of a genius over there can't get it right no matter how many times I've told him?, thought Alberta. She hoped it wasn't just her – that Russell forgot a lot of girls. On the other hand, she thought she'd be special to him, in some perverse way, if he only forgot *her* name.

"Here's the thing, Mr. Greenblatt –"

"Call me Sid, doll."

Alberta explained to Sid that the avatar wasn't like most avatars. Not only wasn't it anchored to her computer, it wasn't even like a projected hologram – which would have been pretty advanced – but that Russell felt like flesh, blood and bone (she left out the 'semen' part). He was just like a real person, only... he wasn't.

"Whoa, Nellie!" Sid shouted. "Really? Bring him here."

Alberta explained that Russell couldn't leave the apartment, at least not yet.

As it turned out, Sid still drove his '66 Buick and he lived only two freeway exits away from her. Greenblatt said he'd be there in 15 minutes.

As soon as they all logged off, Alberta went into the bathroom to fix her hair and put some makeup on. She gently suggested that Russell might want to wash his face, brush his teeth with one of the three unopened toothbrushes she had bought him, and otherwise make himself look presentable.

Russell just laughed. "Sid's seen me buck naked at 90 pounds, strung out on STP after a 10-day fast camping out at the Salton Sea. He'll be fine."

Besides, Russell was busy writing lyrics to something that he said, when he finished it, would blow everyone's mind to the point of no return. Like JFK.

Within the aforementioned 15 minutes, there was a knock on the door. It was an old guy with long, crazy, white hair, the eye-patch in place, and tattoos covering his saggy skin: None other than Sid Greenblatt.

Alberta shook his frail hand and walked him inside.

Russell was sitting down, playing guitar. Sid went up to him and they hugged, vigorously patting each other's backs. The old man wheezed, the wind knocked out of him. Then he said, "My god. You *are* real…"

Alberta went back to configuring the recording software.

Russell didn't reply. He was excited to play what he'd been writing, and Sid was happy to sit at the foot of the bed and listen to his client and best friend for the first time since 1971.

"Dig this, Siddy."

With insistent strumming on his new guitar, Russell sang:

> *Join me, my friends, my guests*
> *On the Never Ending Cosmic Tour*
> *Humanity's mantra*
> *For the ultimate quest*
> *Join me in this endeavor*
> *Because together, we'll live forever*
> *Digits meet digits*
> *Atoms meet Atoms*
> *Heads meet the Mindhead*
> *And the undead*
> *In the field beyond all possibilities*
> *Past the insanity we call reality*
> *I'll meet you there…*

"Goldstein," Sid gasped. "That was fucking beautiful!"

"Thanks, man." He winked. "You're the only one who can call me Goldstein."

"And you and Claudia are the only ones who can call me Siddy."

Alberta looked up from her coding. "Is Claudia your wife?"

"Yes, ma'am. We've been married for over 40 years."

Russell sat up. "Wait a minute, you're not talking about Crazy Dallas Chick, are you?"

Sid nodded.

Russell set the guitar aside. "Are you out of your fucking mind? After what she did to me?"

Sid was nonplussed. "You ought to be thanking me for saving your life."

Alberta butted in. "I thought I was the one who did that." She was angry, but mostly at herself for feeling jealous of this Claudia woman, who had to be in her 70s, at least.

"No," said Sid pointedly, "You've done the world a favor by bringing Russell back to life. But I'm talking about saving him from Crazy Dallas Chick."

"There you go, Siddy, trying to make yourself a hero. I could've handled it."

"Well there YOU go, Goldstein, you ingrate! You wouldn't have been alive enough for you to die onstage at the Isle of Lucy if it hadn't been for me. As your manager, there was no sex and drugs for me – when I wasn't designing your album covers and making sure there were no green M&Ms backstage, I was keeping CDC from trying to kill you. Remember the time you played *Acid Rain* in

Houston and Claudia rushed the stage and tried to throw battery acid in your face? I lost an eye because of you!"

"Wait, guys," said Alberta. She turned to Russell. "Is that why you never played *Acid Rain* after the Houston show?"

"That's right," snapped Sid. "Even this genius here, who also happens to be a pansy, could easily have performed the song again after I took care of her."

"Crazy Dallas Chick?" asked Russell. "What do you mean you took care of her?"

"You know damn well what I mean. I married her in the summer of '71. Took the bullet for you, man. It's been a living hell."

Russell shook his shaggy head. "Trippy, man." Then it was back to business. "Siddy, did you bring those lyrics?"

Sid reached into the front pocket of his plaid golf pants, and handed Russell a folded-up, yellowed piece of mimeographed notebook paper.

Russell carefully opened it, read the lyrics to himself, then turned to Alberta. "Baby, is the tape recorder set up?"

She checked all the connections from the guitar and mic to the computer. "Looks like it."

Russell started strumming again. "It's the cosmic tour…"

In spite of his frail frame, Sid bumped Alberta off to the side and took over the controls on the computer. "Keep singing, yeah, that's it," he said encouragingly to Russell. "We can live-stream on YouTube and Facebook so everyone can hear."

"I don't think that's a good idea," fretted Alberta, trying to switch the controls back on her computer.

While Alberta and Sid wrestled with the software, Russell got into his own bag and played and sang louder and louder.

"Let go of my laptop!" she yelled at Sid.

Sid elbowed her with a sharp jab. "Keep singing, Russell, keep singing! The world needs you! The world needs your help!"

"No, Russell! Now isn't the time. I have to save you online, remember?"

"This fat pig isn't going to save anyone. Keep playing, Russell!"

"Don't call her that!" Russell glared at Sid, but it was true: He was a pansy. So, he didn't press the point. Russell went back to singing and turned up the dials all the way – he couldn't hear himself over the melee.

The trio fought over the computer and as Russell got closer and closer to the mic screaming, "It's the never-ending cosmic tourrrr!" suddenly, there was a spark and Russell's body shook in electric spasms and then seized up.

Alberta and Sid's three eyes went temporarily blind in a blast of white.

In a flash, Russell was gone!

Blinking, Alberta and Sid looked at each other and then at the bed.

All that was left of Russell was his guitar, his newly-written lyrics, the leather vest, and some Twinkies he'd hidden in the pockets.

"Now look what you've done," Alberta seethed at Sid through gritted teeth.

"Yeah," he said, looking at the computer. "Now look what I've done." He jabbed at the screen with an age-yellowed fingernail, where they could see, in the 720 x 480 widescreen video viewing box, Russell was onstage performing at the Isle of Lucy. "Russell Aquarius has four billion likes on Facebook right now. That's four billion more likes than you'll ever get. Not to mention the fact I own the rights to all his music." Sid rubbed his hands together in a perfectly creepy mimic of Ebenezer Scrooge.

Alberta stared at the laptop screen. She could only guess that being reunited with his long-lost lyrics, and realizing that Crazy Dallas Chick had transferred her obsession to Sid, Russell's whole molecular structure transmuted into a digital series of ones and zeros and he was now in somewhere on an eternal Cosmic Tour in the ethosphere.

There would be no 'day the music died'… ever.

BONUS TRACK

After he left her apartment that night, on the phone to his accountant as he slipped out the door, Alberta never saw Sid Greenblatt again.

She went to work the next day, and life went on. Nobody seemed to realize or care she was the creator of the avatar that was making new Russell Aquarius music online, and she couldn't prove it since the code went 'poof!' right along with the rocker who burned out but didn't fade away.

Eventually, she took Merrick back. He begged for another chance, realizing how much he loved her after the guy who answered her phone told him how special she was (even though this guy had called her by the name "Alabaster"). He even started learning to play guitar to please her. She was flattered, but she didn't agree with the tuning changes Merrick made to the '62 Gibson Hummingbird. But at least he put the toilet seat back down after using it.

It was lonely without Russell there. After a few days of grieving, Alberta tried to recreate the avatar, but with no success. Sometimes, just for old times' sake, she'd spritz her skin with patchouli oil and pleasure herself. Alberta didn't want to admit it, but she missed that lovable and sexy dead guy. She could tune into his YouTube and Facebook pages anytime she wanted, but it wasn't the same. He was no longer interactive. He was just playing that Isle of Lucy concert, on the Cosmic Tour forever and ever.

One day, she decided to read the comments listed underneath the video. There were thousands and thousands of them, and Russell's pages were up millions more followers. She scrolled through the posts, mostly from star-struck wannabe groupies, and teenage boys who idolized the dead-alive rocker. But suddenly, she stopped scrolling.

Her eyes widened in disbelief.

There was a comment from a user who called himself "FurryFreakAngel1." It said, simply, "Dearest Alberta: Thank you for your hospitality, your inspiration, and your sexuality. I'll never forget you, and I'll love you forever and beyond. Yours, Russell."

Alberta was on cloud nine.

Russell finally remembered her name.

LITTLE ROSIE VS. THE DEVIL

By Staci Layne Wilson

Little Rosie remembered when she was a tree.

She sprouted, from just a tiny seedling, over a century ago in Karnataka. As she grew, kissed by the sun and nourished by the rain, she provided protection and shelter. She was shade for the delicate coffee plants that flourished near her roots, and this made her very happy. She loved nothing more than to sing: she did so, as the breeze rustled through her leaves and tickled her fragrant flowers.

The Shisham Rosewood took pride in knowing India's shade-grown beans were legendary all over the world, because of her. The resulting coffee was unusually tasty and robust, since the plants flourished in a natural ecosystem with native flora and fauna. They took root in her leaf mulch, and were fertilized by the birds flitting in her branches and the bugs burrowing in her bark.

It seemed her life would never end, as the seasons came and went. Hundreds of them: sun, rain, wind.

When she felt the cut of the chainsaw, she wanted to scream. To cry. To ask, "Why?"

What would happen to her now? Would she be chopped up and burned to cinders in a fireplace? Made into formal dining chairs? Would she be reduced to veneer paneling on the walls of some boring office building?

Her sap tears flowed. Never again would she see her beautiful home under the blue sky. It was all over.

Being sectioned, stowed, then shipped – it was all a blur to her.

Finally, she realized what was happening when she heard voices. As a conscious creature of nature, language was no barrier to her understanding.

She would be made into a guitar. She remembered, on occasion, when boys would sit at her roots, plucking at their instruments. Sometimes she talked to these former trees, now cut and shaped, glued, fitted with frets, strings, and swathed in finishing shellac. The guitars didn't seem to mind not being trees anymore; maybe she'd feel the same.

But what if she was never played? What if some thoughtless kid bought her on a whim, banged away at her for a while, stuck her in a dark attic, and forgot all about her? It was her worst fear.

Little Rosie needn't have fretted... if you'll pardon the pun. She was made into one of the most beautiful and coveted of her kind – a Fender Telecaster, hand carved by a master luthier in 1969. Some said her solid body was too heavy and her sound overly bright, but Little Rosie was rare and beautiful. She was one of the few whose neck and body came from the same tree.

Everybody wanted her, but she was given as a gift to a musician who truly treasured her. His name was Strings McGee, and he took great care of her. She slept nestled in a bed of blue velvet enclosed in a hard-case bound in alligator leather, and whenever he played her, it was – she imagined – like being made love to.

"Oh, please," scoffed the guitar called The Duck. "What sentimental fool you are, Little Rosie. *Love*, indeed!"

Little Rosie knew she shouldn't have said anything at all, but she was bored. Backstage, waiting to be played with several other famous guitars, there wasn't much else to do but share one's feelings. And on occasion, treasured memories.

It was said that guitars became the extensions of their strummers, and sometimes even took on the personalities of their people.

The Duck belonged to hotshot, hot-shit neo-classical metal-head, Yngwie Malmsteen. He was a cream-colored Stratocaster, made in 1971. Little Rosie couldn't blame The Duck for having an attitude. After all, he hadn't been treated very kindly. He'd had several pickup changes, new frets put in after a so-called fan threw a bottle at his body, and his neck had been replaced at least six times after headstock breakage thanks to Yngwie throwing him up into the air and failing to catch him. He'd crashed to the hard floor of the stage so many times, it was no wonder The Duck was damaged more than just physically.

Eric Clapton's Blackie was propped up on a stand nearby. Blackie was kind of a Franken-guitar. He was built using the best parts of three different 1956 Strats Clapton bought at Sho-Bud, a little specialty store in Nashville. He purchased six altogether, then gave the remaining three to his friends Steve Winwood, George Harrison, and Pete Townsend.

Little Rosie prayed that she would never, ever wind up in the grasp of temperamental Townsend... a pile of splinters would be all that was left.

"Don't let The Duck get you down," Blackie said, gently. "I know how you feel, Little Ro. It's the most beautiful thing in the world, to be played by hands that know your body intimately."

"Thank you," the rosewood guitar sighed, with a quiet, nearly imperceptible twang of her G-string.

Trigger, Willie Nelson's old, beat up Martin N20 sat there too, reeking softly of bud and etched hard by her years of experience. She stayed silent, while Keith Richard's Micawber, a '53 Telecaster, couldn't help bragging about how he had more to do with the sound of *Honky Tonk Women* and *Brown Sugar* than Keef himself.

"No, it's a team effort," argued The First Wife, a 1961 chocolate sunburst Stratocaster belonging to Stevie Ray Vaughan.

Duane Edddy's hollow-body Gretsch joined the fray, and even Nancy Wilson's Nighthawk chimed in.

Eventually, Little Rosie tuned them out. As the sound-check for the big jam commenced, she thought back to her first crush. He was a red double-neck Gibson EDS-1275, and he had no name. He didn't need one. From the moment virtuoso Jimmy Page picked him up and played *Stairway to Heaven*, the instrument had only to be seen and heard to be known.

Little Rosie and the Gibson went on tour together in 1977. It began inauspiciously enough on April Fool's Day at the Dallas Memorial Auditorium. A luxurious a 45-seat Boeing 707 called Caesar's

Chariot took them from city to city, finally finishing up three months later in Oakland, and ending in the tragedy.

But the trials and tribulations of humans meant little to Rosie. She had lived over 100 years, and would go on at least a hundred more (if Townsend didn't get a hold of her).

Little Rosie knew she was no dog. From her headstock decals, string tees, bridge and saddle, hardware, finish, pickups, knobs and her sheer weight – "like a collapsed star," Strings sometimes complained after a long set – she was a rare thing of beauty. But the Gibson double-neck was an entity unto himself. Like her, he wasn't a stock model. He was a custom-made cherry 6/12 and had a slightly different shape, and one-piece mahogany necks instead of the three-piece maple, and tailpieces positioned near the bottom of his body, increasing sustain.

But Led Zeppelin didn't sustain, and that 1977 tour was their last. Little Rosie never saw or heard the Gibson again.

But his stories were enough to keep Rosie enthralled for the rest of her days. The things he'd seen, and the superstar guitars he'd met!

"I knew a guitar who was possessed by the Devil himself," he once told her.

"Really?" she marveled. "Who?"

"He was an old-timer. A Gibson, like me. He was a beat-up old Kalamazoo Archtop owned by none other than Robert Johnson, the bluesman from Mississippi. It happened back in the 1930s… Archie was there, the day the Devil came to meet Johnson at the Crossroads. He claimed he took the Devil into himself to save his master, but in end his sacrifice was futile."

Like so many other musicians – Jimi Hendrix, Janis Joplin, Jim Morrison, Russell Aquarius, Kurt Cobain… Robert Johnson died at the age of 27. There was no saving him from the clutches of Satan.

Little Rosie found the story fascinating, but she didn't believe it.

She didn't believe it, until the night the Devil came to her with an offer.

It was years and years after the '77 tour. Years and years after any tour. Strings was finished. Fingers cramped with knots, heart broken by a life on the road with nothing to show for it but a chain of ex-wives, child support payments, song rights written away, and a mountain of debt. Little Rosie was put away, forgotten… just as she had originally feared.

She was alone, drowsy and void of spirit, when one night she heard a seductive whisper.

"Wake up, Little Rosie…"

Her strings tensed.

"You miss it, don't you? The songs, the applause, the love, the adulation. Remember when you were in the spotlight? When you were worshipped?"

"Who's there?" she breathed.

"Me… the one who comes at the 11th hour, the one to soothe your despair, the one to bring you back onstage."

"…Satan?"

Her case slowly opened. Little Rosie peered out. Strings was sitting on his sofa in what she guessed was an alcoholic stupor, and all was quiet.

Next to her was an indistinct black swirl, a sentient being of the underworld. Somehow, it smiled. "Well, aren't you a pretty girl?" he declared, all seduction and flattery.

Little Rosie stayed quiet.

"Strings already told me he wants the deal... but since you two share a soul, I wouldn't be so rude as to just go ahead without your OK."

"Well, aren't you the upstanding citizen?" Rosie sneered, using her low-E string to convey her menace.

The murky figure formed into something more corporeal, and reached into the case.

Little Rosie bristled, driving a splinter into the Devil's grasping palm.

"Owww! That hurts," he cried, bringing his soft hand to his mouth.

"Try it again, and I'll pop a tuning peg right into your eye!"

Strings stirred, and blinked. He looked over at the open guitar case. He shook his head, quizzically. "Hm, how'd that get unlocked?" he muttered. But aside from mild curiosity, the guitarist didn't seem at all alarmed or troubled.

"You weren't telling me the truth, were you?" hissed Little Rosie. "Strings can't even see you."

Satan shrugged. "They don't call me the Father of Lies for nothing."

Little Rosie conjured up every bit of love and respect she had for Strings, willing him to come to her.

Strings, as if in a trance-state, got up and went to the open guitar case. Still, he saw nothing but Little Rosie.

"He's mine," she said to the Devil. "You can't have him."

Wound tight, she popped her A-String and the end of it caught Satan like a whip on the tip of his hooked nose.

"Ouch! You *bitch*!" the dark deity yelped, just before disappearing in a puff of sulphurous smoke.

Strings reached in, and picked Little Rosie up. "I haven't been taking very good care of you, have I?" he said, stroking her dark finish, polishing her pickguard with his sleeve, and examining the broken string. He strummed, and she rose to meet his touch… together, they wrote a new song, and as the days turned to weeks, that song became an LP.

Strings called the album *Little Rosie vs. The Devil*. He thought of himself as the evil one, for neglecting her for so long and forgetting the true power of music. That was partially true, but Rosie knew better – and because she and Strings did indeed share a soul, the gifted guitarist rediscovered his true self without having to sell anything but his songs.

The world, in spite of its Devils, knows good soul (and rock 'n roll) when it hears it. *Little Rosie vs. The Devil* went straight to a rather heavenly Number 1. Strings regained his fame and fortune, and Little Rosie was never forgotten again.

IN(TER)VENTION

By Darren Gordon Smith

I.

Invention #1

He was late and he knew it. He was also drunk, and knew that, too. How else could he have been expected to get through an excruciating evening with Mom and Song without first stopping for three fingers of rye? And how was he to know – for he had never been to The Palsied Pup before – that he would get there just as Happy Hour was starting? And that he could afford two g & t's for the price of one?

Though he was as frugal as ever, it seemed unwise not to take advantage of an offer like that.

It's not like they paid him nearly enough at that cheap digital rag to even nurse a $4 Bud during the insufferable concerts and talent shows they'd make him review. Luckily, he carried a flask, just in case he had to watch yet another derivative band preening around as if they'd invented the three chords that inevitably would make up their set.

Now, after a dozen or so drinks, he was fortified and ready to do his duty: to see his folks. He'd taken a train and a bus all the way out to the hinterlands of Seward in the pouring rain. And now, after leaving the bar, he still had a two mile walk just to get to their place.

To pass the time, he hummed Blind Melon's *No Rain*, Bob Marley's *Misty Morning*, and Johnny Cash's *Five Feet High and Rising*. He rattled his brain to remember some of his other favorite songs about rain. He cursed himself for losing his iPad at The Hoary Chestnuts set last night. Oh well, he'd just have to conjure his favorite tunes in his head, just like Lester Bangs and Leonard Feather, and all the great music journalists of yore.

Ian was soaking wet and exhausted by the time he got to Mom and Song's mansion. OK, he'd often admit to his drinking buddies, it's not really a mansion. But it *was* a big house. And its ostentation, like the circular driveway he was walking up, never set well with him. Especially now that he was broke again. Mud, silt, and pebbles found their way into his holey sneakers. If Mom and Song weren't so stingy with their money, he thought, trudging the stone path to the porch, he could finally get a good pair of boots.

He stood at the imposing set of 10-foot high doors and rapped on a brass knocker. He expected his mother, or Song, or maybe their housekeeper Natty, to open the door. Instead it was Dean, Larry's husband, who greeted him. What was he doing here? This was supposed to be a quiet dinner with his mom and step-dad. Then, after dessert, Ian planned to ask them for another loan.

But before he even entered the parlor (his mother's name for the spacious living room) he sensed that something was up. Dean was normally a high testosterone, Army and law enforcement type of gay guy. But now he was somber and subdued. Dean paused before opening the door. He scratched his flat-top and said, in an irritatingly soothing voice, "Ian, Mom and Dad and your brother have invited a few us here to talk to you."

With a flourish, Dean opened the door to reveal a group of people sitting in a semicircle. Mom and Song were there, of course, both offering sad smiles. And there was Ian's brother, Larry. Two of Ian's cousins were there, as was his Step-Uncle Chen. Also present were two classmates Ian hadn't seen since kindergarten, almost twenty years ago. Finally, there were three strangers – an abnormally skinny teenage girl, a bloated middle aged man, and a tiny, shriveled nonagenarian of indeterminate gender.

The middle-aged stranger held out his hand and said, "We wish you well, Aidan," and gave him a kiss on the mouth.

"His name is Ian," Missy corrected the man. As Ian extricated himself from the stranger, Missy whispered to her intoxicated son, "Take a seat over there," pointing to the center of the semi-circle. Ian looked around for a chair but found none; was he supposed to sit on the floor at their feet?

Step-Uncle Chen brought in a folding chair from the garage, put it at the center of the semi-circle, and motioned for Ian to sit. He did.

Missy continued. "You need to listen to what we have to say. Larry, tell him."

"We have certain concerns about you, and Dean, as you may know, has been studying for the past year and is about to get his license as an Interventionist."

Dean cleared his throat. "InterveNOR."

Ian raised an eyebrow. "So, you're going to lead an intervention before even getting certified?"

"Correct-a-mundo," said Dean.

"And is this your first one?"

"That's none of your business," said Dean.

"Ian," said Larry, "There's no need for you to get defensive."

"I'm not getting defensive. If anyone is getting defensive, it's —"

"Clearly, you're being defensive," Larry pointed a finger at Ian, "And passive-aggressive too, so just drop it." Ian hated his brother's pop-psych power plays but decided to let it go. In Ian's more rational moments like this, he knew there was no arguing with his sanctimonious and none-too-bright sibling.

Dean straddled a metal folding chair, cleared his throat and declared, "Let's roll!" This may have been Dean's first intervention, but the burly former police officer and Army drill sergeant quickly took charge of things.

Ian counted a dozen people surrounding him. He felt like Jesus, except none of those present were his disciples. And, unlike the Son of God, Ian knew that not one, but ALL of these people would betray him. Most already had.

"OK, folks, let's get busy!" said Dean. The Intervenor leaned on the back of his chair and pounded his fist with peremptory authority. "OK, we have a quorum. Now, unless anyone, EXCEPT the Intervenee — and that means *you*, Ian — has any objection to the commencement of these proceedings, let the Intervention begin!" He rang a tinkly bell.

Ian, sensing Dean's extreme earnestness, took another look at the motley crew that had been assembled. He let out a chuckle. Then he made a serious face of his own and turned to his mother. "Is this intervention about my lateness problem?"

"No, dear," said Missy, "It's –"

"Or my *earliness* problem? You know, premature ejaculation?"

"Heavens, no. We didn't even –"

"Oh, I know! Is it because of my chronic fingernail biting?"

"No, son –"

"My vintage Arabian porn collection?"

"No, we don't care about –"

"I'm just kidding, I don't have one; my smut's all new. Plus, I'm not that into horses." He pretended to wrack his brain. "Oh, I get it now. I didn't even think you guys knew. This intervention is because I'm becoming left-handed, right? I was already thinking of seeing a shrink about that my ambidexterity."

"Sweetheart, no –"

"Is it my poison pen review of Taylor Swift's *1989*?" The visitors looked confused, but Ian gave them bitter laugh. "Sorry, I was just joking. Of course you would never read anything I write." He furrowed his brow into a frown. "But seriously, folks, is it because I'm short?" He stood five-foot-seven though, no shorter than his brother or Chen. Missy shook her head.

"Is it because of the way I dress?" He was wearing a fedora hat, a London Fog trench coat, and a t-shirt underneath which advertised the Cameron Crowe film *Almost Famous*. Every article of clothing he had on was soaked.

"No," said Larry. "But it's pretty corny, especially for someone who fancies himself a writer."

Ian ignored his brother. "Is it my auto-repetitive mastication syndrome?"

"Your WHAT?" Mom asked.

Ian loudly chomped his teeth.

"Don't get smart with your mother!" barked Song. Normally, he was a quiet, almost mute older gentleman. But when provoked, Song reverted to the tough-as-nails Marine Corps captain he'd been before his retirement two decades ago.

Larry said, "Ian, we're all here because we need to talk to you about your drinking and how it is affecting you and those who love you."

Ian wondered who those loving individuals might be, but chose to bite his tongue.

"That's right, we heard your drinking sucks!" said a tinny voice coming from a laptop computer that lay open on the coffee table.

Ian leaned forward to look at the monitor. There were dozens of people each on their own webcam, displayed in a moving slide show in three rows of three. It looked like the Brady Bunch on the Hollywood Squares playing Chat Roulette. Ian couldn't tell which one of the talking heads had just spoken. In fact, he didn't recognize any of the faces who appeared on the screen. The whole online set up struck Ian as ludicrous. He let out a snort.

Dean smiled, oblivious to Ian's derision. "Pretty cool, huh? There's this site on the Internet that conducts virtual interventions."

Ian was trying, really he was, to be civil. He just wanted to get the whole thing over with so he could make it back in time to meet up with friends for drinks at The Second Opinion, a neighborhood bar, catty-corner from Seward Memorial Hospital. But he couldn't suppress another laugh. To Ian, the term "virtual" went out with Electronic Bulletin Boards, Megabyte Mondays, AOL and LOL.

"Cyber-virtual interventions, huh?" Ian said to Dean. "What will they think of next? Chat rooms?"

Dean's already tight smile turned to a grimace. He wasn't one of those friendly, big smile guys by nature. But Dean looked like he was trying his best to be personable and caring, skills this Intervenor gig apparently required.

"OK!" Dean peered around the room to see if there were any African Americans in the room. There were none. "Let's call a spade a spade. Buddy, your drinking stinks and you're a goddam alkie –"

Missy cut in. "I think, well, what Dean is trying to say –"

"Please, Mom," her son-in-law interjected. "Address me as The Intervenor."

"As you wish. Anyway, what The InterveNOR is saying is that we are all concerned, Ian. We're worried about what you are doing to yourself, what with all the wine, vodka, and who knows what else."

"How about the gin and tonics whenever I crank up Oasis? Do they count too?" Ian asked helpfully.

All eyes turned to Dean. "Without resorting to the Interventionor's Manual, then I'm just shooting from the hip, but I'd say they probably count."

"Of course they count!" said Missy. "But I love you. WE love you. And we're just worried sick about you."

"Because," said Larry, who had a knack for stating the obvious, "We don't like what your drinking is doing to you."

Ian paused. "I think I'm starting to get the picture. So, is there a consensus here that my responsible enjoyment of alcoholic beverages has a deleterious effect on me and everyone around me?"

"Yes!" was the chorus from everyone in the room. Some tinny voice on the Brady Bunch monitor yelled, "Praise Jesus!" Another tinny voice asked what "deleterious" meant.

Ian sunk toward the floor, feigning ignorance and embarrassment. "I understand completely now. I guess I just never knew that drinking to excess was bad."

Ian thought about telling these fools that, for every Bon Scott, John Bonham, and F. Scott Fitzgerald, there were millions of other heavy drinkers who are exceedingly happy. But Ian was cornered and he knew it. These pinheads, led by the grand wizards of pinheads – Larry and Dean – wouldn't be satisfied until Ian quit doing the one thing he enjoyed. The only thing that helped him deal with spending even a single hour with his revolting family.

"Ian, you say you understand?" asked Dean.

"Yes. And I think we should look into rehab," said Ian.

The members of the group smiled and everyone high fived each other, except for Step-Uncle Chen, who spoke no English and really had no idea what was going on.

"Oh, and thank you all for caring." Ian started to fidget.

Dean was obviously pleased with himself. "How's that for one-stop therapy, huh?" he asked the group.

Dean answered his own question by adding, "Pretty darn good if I do say so myself."

Suddenly Ian doubled over in pain. "I'm sorry," he said, through clenched teeth, "But my bladder is bursting. It's been one heck of a long trip. Excuse me for a moment." He stood up, though not quite erect, held his bladder, and waddled out to the bathroom.

Actually he did need to pee, but not that bad. Ian had a more important reason to leave the group than urination. And that reason had nothing to do with popping a squat, either. Ian lifted the toilet seat and did his business. But he didn't flush. Keeping the light and the overhead fan on, he crept out of the bathroom, silently closing the door.

Then he snuck into Song's study. The light was off but Ian knew his way around Song's sacred little room in the dark well enough to get to the closet. That's where the old man kept his guns. Ian found the steel box that held the firearms, but the damned thing had a padlock and chain around it. Then he found a wooden chest with its top left open. Ian took out his cellphone to illuminate its contents: an assortment of knives, daggers, swords, scythes, and machetes. He almost sliced his thumb trying to dig into the box to look for more.

Finally, Ian found something that would do the trick: a rusty, old dagger with a razor sharp edge.

He got back on his feet. But he stood up too soon and felt woozy. Though he was dizzy and disoriented, he was determined to end it all right then and there.

He tried to direct the blade into the side of his neck. But his vertigo got the best of him. He slipped, dropped the knife, and fell to the ground. He found himself flat on his back, with the knife planted firmly between his shoulder blades. He tried to move so he could bend his arm back and release the knife, but the weapon only dug in even further, piercing skin and muscle. When the knife hit a nerve ending, Ian let out a piercing, anguished cry.

Hearing this, the group of interventionists ran to the bathroom, to the bedrooms, and finally to Song's study.

Dean turned the lights on to reveal the bloody scene before them. Fortunately, the middle-aged stranger, Ken, was a paramedic. (He was a new neighbor who'd been invited over by Missy after he mentioned that he'd been to a couple interventions in the past and enjoyed the food.) Ken immediately examined Ian's injuries. The poor young man was still clinging to life. Ken staunched the blood and called an ambulance. Then he gave Ian mouth-to-mouth resuscitation, notwithstanding the fact that Ian was breathing normally. Since Ken said he had some pull with the city's ambulance services, they came within 90 seconds, instead of the 45-minute wait that was typical for their area.

The first responders turned Ian on his side and put him on a stretcher, leaving the knife in his shoulder for fear of causing further blood loss if they removed it. Ken sat in the back of the ambulance and continued to give Ian mouth-to-mouth, until one of the EMTs told him to knock it off.

The reason the knife landed where it did, instead of Ian's neck – in other words, the reason he lived, instead of hitting his jugular vein or an artery and dying immediately – was simple, at least to Ian: he had survived BECAUSE of his drinking. Had Ian not been feeling the effects of Happy Hour he wouldn't have been dizzy and slipped, and therefore the knife did not reach its intended target.

II.

Invention #2

Yes, Ian's alcoholism saved him. Sort of.

Once he was rushed to the hospital, he lay in critical condition, fighting for life in the ICU. Missy, Song, Larry, and Dean sped to the hospital, where the four of them nervously sat in the waiting room. The rest of the interventionists stayed at the house, where, in their grief, they decided not to let a Costco vat of red velvet cake ice cream go to waste.

The waiting room was mostly empty except for a couple of families sitting at the other end. The two couples – Song and Missy, Dean and Larry, sat face-to-face in the dim light. The fluorescent lighting was subdued, either to make the room feel tranquil, or perhaps as the hospital's cheap-ass cost cutting measure.

Song held his wife as she sobbed, shook, and caterwauled. "My son! Oh, my son!" She repeated this over and over, to the disapproving glares of the other people in the waiting room. Missy daubed her eyes with a tissue that was already soaked with tears. She leaned forward toward Larry and Dean and asked, "Oh, God, what have we done?" She let out a wail.

"There, there," said her husband, unable to find anything else to say.

"It'll be OK, Mom," said Dean. "It's not uncommon to have unresolved feelings come up during an intervention."

"*Unresolved feelings*?!" cried Song. "Ian – her son... OUR son – is clinging to life right now and this is NOT the time for your intervention psychobabble!"

Larry pressed a finger into Song's chest. "Don't you dare talk to my husband in that tone! It's very disrespectful."

"And it's not very constructive!" said Dean, a little too loudly.

"Both of you, please!" said Missy. "I can't bear this. Oh, why did we do this horrible thing, this stupid intervention? Why couldn't you leave my poor Ian alone?"

"Because, Mother," said Larry, "Ian was killing himself and we couldn't stand by and just watch him make one bad decision after another. Like, him quitting dental school to become a music journalist! Jeez, in a day when journalists can't make a living and newspapers are closing left and right, it's like Ian dove right in after the Titanic and yelled, '*Wait for me!*'" Larry's stupidly jovial face suddenly turned serious. "And most important, Ian was killing himself with alcohol."

"So YOU say, dear. But we went on your word and on Dean's word that Ian had a problem."

"Let's be clear, Missy," said Dean. "I was present solely in my capacity as the Intervenor. I am not, nor can I be, a percipient witness to Ian's drinking. I was called here because Larry asked me to, and I wanted to help..." Dean put his head in his hands and whined to no one in particular, "Jeez-Louise, there are so many liability issues with these things. I knew I should've drawn a contract. Or at least a CYA letter."

"Shut up, Dean," said Larry. "You can't Cover Your Ass this time, so don't try to pin this all on ME. We both know you've seen Ian get tanked before."

"I don't know, maybe once."

"It was definitely more than once," said Larry. "So cut the shit."

"Language!" said Song. "You know better than to talk like that in front of your mother."

"How's this for language?" Larry asked his step-father. "Fuck. You."

"Oh, *yeah*? Well fuck you, too!" Song stiffened, as if he were expecting a salute in return. "Don't forget, I can still bend you over my knee and spank you, young man."

"Step-Daddy, I'm not a child anymore," said Larry, "Haven't you noticed?"

"I wouldn't know, by the way you're acting," said Song.

"Larry, please," said Missy, "Just stop it! You ARE being childish. You're a grown man for Pete's sake, you're 33 years old."

"I'm 34. You ought to know your own son's age!"

"Oh, Larry. I'm ashamed of you, making this big fuss while your poor brother is back there clinging to life…" She blew her nose again. "Oh, poor, pathetic little Ian."

"Mother, that's poppycock! My 'poor brother' wouldn't be clinging to life if it weren't for your husband's collection of weapons!"

Song's face shot a fiery red. The vein running up and down his forehead pulsated. He held his breath and searched for the right words to express his anger at his insolent step-son.

Dean beat him to the punch. "Now wait a minute, Larry, dear. This is a Live Free or Die issue so I don't really think you should be criticizing your father –"

"STEP-father."

"Whatever." Dean scratched his head. "But there's absolutely nothing wrong with knives. Or guns. Everyone knows that knives don't kill people–"

"Save it," said Larry. "We've heard this all before: 'Guns don't kill people. Only people kill people.' And only people kill people – with guns, knives, and bombs."

Both Dean and Song looked confused.

"Well, anyway," said Dean, "I'm just saying that you can't fault Dad –"

"Stop calling him 'Dad'!" said Larry. "He's not YOUR Dad! And he's not MINE either. He's not anyone's dad. He's a non-dad with children. Kind of like a reverse bastard, I guess you could say."

"Larry!" cried Missy. "You will not be naughty like that. Song has been your daddy since you were 12 years old."

Larry looked sheepish.

"As I was saying," said Dean, "There's nothing wrong with Dad – or Song, if you will – having a knife collection OR a gun collection." Dean stopped to scratch behind his ear. "That said, and I'm not being critical, but it is a legitimate question as to whether it was negligent or not to maintain a collection of lethally sharp blades in your home without safely locking them up."

"What did I just hear?!" bellowed Song. "When you're treading on my Second Amendment rights conferred by the Almighty, you're treading on thin ice, pals'y."

Missy wiped her nose with another soaked tissue. "Honey, please don't get angry, but Dean's got a point. You can't just leave your guns and knives lying around like that."

"I didn't leave my firearms lying around!" Song banged his fist on the end table next to him. A 10-year-old Reader's Digest and one of the doctor's yachting magazines fell to the floor. "Those blessed guns WERE locked up! And the knives – I wasn't expecting to have this intervention in my house –"

"OUR house," said Missy, "It's not just yours."

Song took a deep breath. "I know, dear. I misspoke, OK?"

"Boy, I'll say," said Larry.

Song ignored him. "Missy, sweetheart. It's just that I didn't want to do this thing at our house."

"And you think I did? I wouldn't have had it at our place, either, or anywhere, if Larry and Dean hadn't MADE me do it!"

"Mom," said Dean, "Nobody made you do anything. It's not like we came over and put a knife to your throat –" Missy winced at the imagery of that cliché. Dean seemed unaware. "Nor did we put a gun to your head –"

Missy let out a sharp cry. "Stop!!!!! Just stop it! Oh, poor Ian! My poor, poor son!"

"I'm sorry, Mom," said Dean, "I didn't mean it to come out like that."

"Yes, you did. You and Larry are always trying to hurt me."

"No we're not." said Larry. He paused. He wanted to be truthful to his mother. "At least not most of the time."

Song pointed his finger at Larry and Dean. "And you don't think that your stupid intervention – and what it did to Ian – didn't hurt your mother?"

"Hey, that's a cheap shot," said Dean. "Nobody expected this to happen."

"YOU didn't expect it," said Song, "Because you'd never conducted an intervention before. Oh, for the love of God, you don't even have your license yet! Dean, you clearly didn't know WHAT you were doing. And, without even being a licensed Interventionist –"

"I'm an Intervenor!"

"– you used our Ian as a guinea pig."

"A GUINEA? YOU'RE CALLING ME A GUINEA?!" yelled Dean, who'd lost part of his hearing when he was an Army sharpshooter. "I may have Italian blood in me but I'm 100% American, I'll have you know!"

"I didn't call you a guinea. I used the term, *guinea pig* –"

"See?!" yelled Dean, in a voice that everyone in the waiting room could hear. "He's using that word again!"

"I heard it, too!" said Larry, though his hearing was normal. "And he's calling you, a decorated police officer, a *pig*!"

"That's enough, Larry," Song said, "You're just begging to be disciplined!"

"Yeah, and I'll press charges if you do! And anyway, where do you get off saying my husband doesn't know what he's doing? Dean is smarter than you and Mom put together!"

"If Dean's so smart," asked Song, "How come he's hiding behind a mask of stupidity?"

"I will not sit here and have you making homophobic comments about my sweet, smart, and brave husband!"

"I'm not saying anything homophobic, you asshole." Song felt the sudden urge to spit on his step-son.

"Language, please!" said Missy.

"*Language*?!" yelled Song. "Oh, I got to be like, 'I no speaky Engrish,' is that it? Like I'm your little Asian rickshaw driver? Well, I got news for you, Missy: this Korean slash Chinese American is every bit as American as you are!"

Missy fished another Kleenex out of her purse and wiped her eyes.

"You can't talk to Mom that way!" cried Dean.

"She's not your mother," said Song.

"And she's not yours, either!" Dean knew he wasn't making sense but was too angry to care. "And no one was making fun of your ethnicity or questioning your patriotism. You know you're just talking bull –, well, out of respect for Mom, you're talking gobbledygook."

"Gook?" Song yelled. "Did I just hear you call me a gook?" Song jumped up, and got in Dean's face. "How dare, you, sir! I will not stand for any racism, nor will I allow this insolence –from you or from anyone. Not when I was out defending this country, defending YOUR freedoms in 'Nam."

Dean stood up and pounded his chest. "Yeah, well, I was in the Army, too!"

"The Army, ha! A bunch of pansies. I'm Semper Fi."

"So I'm not just a faggot to you, I'm a pansy now?!" Dean was so angry all you could see were the whites of his eyes. "You wanna step outside and see who the real pansy is?!"

"Alright, both of you," said Larry, "Let's just cool it. And Song – "

"I've told you a million times to call him 'Dad'," said Missy.

"Alright, Mom. *Dad!* Enough with the homophobic slurs!"

"How dare you talk to me like that, you disgrace of a step-son." Song reached into his jacket to grab his pistol. "Your brother NEVER would've spoken to me like that." He paused to load his gun. Then he yelled out, "Now, here's a bullet for the next scoundrel who calls me a homophobe!"

Three people at the other end of the room noticed the short man holding a firearm above his head and ran for their lives.

"Two can play that game," said Dean, reaching into his holster to grab his Lugar.

"That's it!" said Larry. He stood up and buttoned his jacket. "I've had it with both of you. I'm going outside for a goddam smoke."

"Not without cleaning your mouth with soap and water first!" said Missy.

Larry ignored her and left the room.

With Larry out of the way, Song pointed his gun directly at Dean, who pointed his at Song. The older man asked, in a voice loud enough for even the hospital staff to hear, "WHO DO I HAVE TO KILL AROUND HERE TO PROVE FOR THE

LAST TIME THAT I AM NOT A HOMOPHOBE?!"

Missy sunk in her chair.

Within minutes a security guard came and ordered Song and Dean to put their weapons away. Missy looked to the ground, silently whimpering. She hated the irascible side effects of her husband's heart medicine.

The security guard, a small, round, older lady, walked Song and his step-son-in-law to the hospital parking lot. There they saw Larry, who was pacing and nervously toking on an e-cigarette. The guard told Song and Dean that, as per hospital protocol, she was required to inspect their weapons and to log their serial numbers. Sensing their apprehension, she assured them that state law forbade her, or any official, from confiscating firearms at a hospital, school, senior center, or church.

Song and Dean still refused to let her inspect their weapons, saying that the whole thing sounded like socialism.

The altercation with the guard escalated, and in the confusion, the two men discharged their weapons. Larry, apparently forgetting that his brother was in the ICU, cried out, "Help me, Ian!" Then all was still. Song, Dean, Larry, and the guard lay in a bloody pool next to a row of doctors' Porsches.

III.

The Writer

In a dark and dingy room, a silhouetted figure of a man with a fedora sits at a desk. Next to him is an ancient Burroughs typewriter, a 100-year-old machine made by the ancestors of *Naked Lunch* author William S. Burroughs. Next to the return tab a burning cigarette rests in between tokes.

The blue glare from his computer monitor gives the writer a ghoulish mien as he furiously types. His features are young; his eyebrows, cynical. If his tweed jacket and winged-tip shoes weren't so dingy he'd resemble his New Journalism heroes Gay Talese and Tom Wolfe.

With a dramatic click of the keyboard, the writer signals to the heavens that he has just finished his requisite two chapters and he's now finished for the night.

He takes a drag off his cancer stick, slides his beat-up Bo Diddley guitar off the bed, and finally downs the last of his gin.

IV.

The Reckoning

Ian awoke to the incessant buzzing of his cellphone. He looked at the clock. It was already past noon. He was supposed to be at his brother's for brunch at 10 o'clock. He could have called Larry to cancel, but Ian was broke and, as usual, he was up for some free food. Luckily, having slept in his clothes, he was already dressed, so he splashed some water on his face, put on his fedora and cabbed it over to Larry's.

As soon as Ian arrived, Larry came out to greet him and to pay the cabbie. Then Larry led Ian inside. Mom and Song were sitting on the couch with stern expressions. Ian was just about to apologize for his tardiness, when Dean came out from the kitchen with a tray of coffee, tea, and pomegranate juice.

"In case you're wondering, Ian," said Dean, "This is an intervention and I'll be your Intervenor for today."

WHAT?! Ian's heart pounded. His mouth went dry. An intervention! And before he even had breakfast and a couple mimosas? This can't really be happening!

Ian looked around the room. "Where is everybody?"

"What do you mean? Who else would be here?" asked Mom.

"Who else cares about you but us?" asked Song.

No one, Ian guessed. His life was sad enough already, and now this?

Ian immediately excused himself and ran into the bathroom. He furiously searched for some method of suicide: pills, razor blades, something to electrocute himself with. But he found nothing. Not even a roll of dental floss to hang himself with. They must've hidden everything before he'd gotten there. The bastards! He tried to sneak out to check the couple's bedroom, when Dean spotted him and escorted him back to the living room.

So now Ian would have to sit through the whole thing: the speeches, the hugs, the torture, all that mealy-mouth stuff. He felt envy for the prisoners at Gitmo – if only they'd just water-board him. Or, better yet, vodka-board him. The whole scene was even worse than he could have ever imagined. And, unlike what he had written the night before, Ian's annoying family stood united as each member prattled on and on about their love and concern for him.

Unable to off himself right then and there, Ian resigned himself to his fate that day. He'd have to just sit there and listen to this shit, just like Bangs being forced to review James Taylor. Or like Dave Marsh, being forced by *Rolling Stone* to slog through a Journey concert. But rather than just sit there and be miserable, Ian decided to use this whole intervention thing as a learning experience.

And what Ian learned that day is that you can't just commit suicide any time you feel like it; things like that take planning. And, most importantly, if you choose to consume large quantities of alcohol on a daily basis, you have to make sure that you completely alienate everyone around you. That way, no one will ever care enough to hold one of these stupid interventions.

DEPRAVED
INDIFFERENCE
By Staci Layne Wilson

Stage One: *Shock*

When I heard Kurt Cobain had committed suicide, I was surprised. This was in '94. I was in middle school.

Yeah, sure: he was a dark, twisted motherfucker. No doubt about that. Just listen to some Nirvana lyrics. Look at who he married. He *had* to have been pretty damn depressed.

But why would someone so young, with so much talent, and a new daughter, kill himself?

At first I thought maybe he just wanted to be in the "27 Club" – so many musicians have died at 27. Morrison, Hendrix and Joplin being the big three. Brian Jones from The Stones, and The Grateful Dead's Pigpen. Amy Winehouse. There's also bluesman Robert Johnson and punker Mia Zapata of The Gits, both of whom were murdered. Even Andy Warhol's protégé Jean-Michel Basquiat kicked off at two-seven. Though Basquiat is way better-known as a painter, he was in a band too.

Some people think Kurt's junkie wife, Courtney Love, talked him into putting that shotgun to his head. Her detractors say she plied him with drugs, including heroin, that she goaded him into it.

But can you really talk someone into suicide? I mean, that's real power.

The note he wrote, found underneath a flower pot in the greenhouse room above his garage – the same place where his body lay for three days before being discovered – quotes a Neil Young song, "It's better to burn out than fade away." He was listening to the *Automatic for the People* album by R.E.M. sometime before he ended it all. At least, that was the CD found in the player.

Right now I'm listening to Nirvana's *Come as You Are*, in which he sings, "...And I swear that I don't have a gun."

Actually, he was a collector. He even had guns as a kid growing up in Washington. Several. People say he hoarded them, people say the police took them away. Whatever the case, I guess he had one too many on that damp April 5th.

I've seen the photos of the scene. There are some fakes out there – for one thing, he didn't blow his face off. If anything he looked peaceful there on the floor, as if resting. The shotgun, a Remington Model 11 20-gauge given to him by his best friend Dylan Carson, lay on his chest. Just a slight trickle of blood could be seen coming from one ear, his features in serene repose. The last words he wrote were, "I love you."

Time to turn the music off and get to work.

I work at a very exclusive museum.

Speaking of Basquiat, we got *Hannibal* back. That's one of his paintings which was stolen, spirited away to Brazil, then recovered. And stolen again. I think it's kind of ugly myself, but Basquiat is one of those painters I admire more than I actually like. I pass the canvass every night on my way to my little office. I'm the one who arranges the private tours. Well, they're all private, actually. Our museum is not open to the public.

The sun is at its most intense now, glowing like an orange coal before trading shifts with the moon. I like this part of the day. It's a good time to start.

Taking my last swallow of Starbucks Thanksgiving blend, I put my chunky mug in the sink and head for the door.

The driver is waiting for me, as usual. He and I are not allowed to speak to one another but we do say hello and goodbye, twice a day. Once at 6PM when he picks me up, and again at 7AM when he drops me off.

The car's windows are tinted darker than is legal, but it's otherwise nondescript. Attention mustn't be drawn to me, or to anyone else who works at the museum.

I slide into the backseat, playing with my iPhone and answering emails during the relatively short ride to LACMA.

We turn right onto Wilshire Boulevard, from Fairfax. The Petersen Automotive Museum is there, its newly unveiled exterior design by Kohn Pedersen Fox Associates giving me a start. I still haven't gotten used to the flashy, almost Gehry-like façade. It used to be kind of charming – a little tacky, even – like the overpriced tourist trap it is. Now it's got these ribbons of stainless steel around three sides and over the top of the deep red building, meant to mimic the streaking speed of a vehicle in full throttle.

Aside from that, the Miracle Mile and L.A.'s Museum Row haven't changed in years. I've been here all my life. My dad held the same position before he retired, died, and I took over; our work is traditional, familial, and fraternal. Not unlike Yale's Skull & Bones Society or even the Freemasons, if I had to draw comparisons.

Traffic is terrible. Crawling along Wilshire, I glance up only occasionally. Mini museums, coffee shops, office buildings. The usual. Only a few people are out and walking about. The sun's gone down and a half moon now hangs casually in the sky, nestled amongst a few wisps of smoggy clouds.

Finally, I'm dropped off. "Goodbye," says the driver. It's the same one, every day I work. I don't know his name, and I never will.

Even in the museum, we have… codenames. Nicknames are more like it. Somebody must know who I really am, though: every Friday, my cover salary shows up electronically wired into my bank account. My real paycheck, the much heftier one, shows up in a numbered the Swiss account of my family (essentially me) every three months without fail.

Still above ground, I head for the LACMA campus, step onto the Resnick North Lawn, and pass beneath the *Levitated Mass*. It's a silly structure passing itself off as art. Not unlike the pyramid in front of The Louvres in Paris – it's just piling stuff on top of stuff. The *Levitated Mass* is a big rock straddling two high walls and people stroll underneath it, thinking it's something special because someone calling himself an artist put it there.

I walk to the front of the museum, where the *Urban Lamps* are illuminated like soft beacons. I like this installation. Several lampposts, all in neat rows and forming a square, make for excellent cover and camouflage as I hide in plain sight, entering the dense forest of metal, glass and light. I stand where I'm supposed to. I flick that familiar, flush switch. Without a sound I'm lowered quickly underground via high-tech trapdoor.

This is the real museum, as far as I'm concerned. The Los Angeles County Museum of Art is just a cover for us. We're windowless of course, but there's an airiness about the place. It smells nice, and it's spacious.

I nod and smile at our receptionist, Lefty. She smiles curtly back. She's an older woman, upper-crust and librarian-like with her blonde bun and her 1960s-era Chanel dress suit – not a hair out of place, not a wrinkle in her skirt. She's looking into her monitor as I go by, headed for my office.

I pass *Hannibal.* I go through the Dutch corridor on my way, as I do every day. I pause to admire Vermeer's *The Concert.* It was stolen in 1990 from the Isabella Stewart Gardner Museum in Boston. News reports say it's from the largest, most catastrophic art theft in world history... I don't know about that. I would say the Vikings, the Romans and the Nazis did some pretty substantial five-finger discounting back in their times.

Basically the same players and setting as Vermeer's *The Music Lesson,* the painting depicts three figures – two women and a man – lit by sunny windowpanes, a black and white marble floor at their feet. A big instrument, a cello I guess, sits in the foreground. It's been reframed, of course. It was cut out of the original. No way around that. We keep our frames simple here, anyway. Almost everything is in plain, thin, straight ebony wood.

Occasionally there's a "break in the case" reported on that particular heist. I always chuckle to myself when I read that – I've got it plugged into my Google notifications. Sometimes, for karma's sake, we give stuff back. But that's only to maintain a cosmic balance of sorts, so we can take something else. We're a superstitious lot.

I was still a kid when this heist took place, but Dad knew all about it before it happened. Hell, for all I know he pulled the strings.

On March 18, 1990, two thieves dressed as police officers and tied up the security guards, smashed frames, tore canvases, and made off with 13 masterpieces, including *The Concert*. There was also a Manet, five drawings by Degas, and three Rembrandts, including his only known seascape, *Storm on the Sea of Galilee*.

That's my favorite. I just glance at most of the other stuff, but there's something so violent and palpably... I don't know... *visceral* about *Storm on the Sea of Galilee*. I have to stop and look at it.

It's such a dynamic piece. There's the delicate ship on the crest of a wicked wave, the dark sky, the determined terror on the faces of the few fighting the mast. There's a man soaked in sea-spray. The others are sitting in quiet resignation on the deck.

I think of it every time I go fishing. (Which isn't as often as I'd like these days.)

I remember once reading about what it's like to drown. I think it was in Sebastian Junger's book, *The Perfect Storm*. It seems horrible and beautiful all at once... it's like the seven stages of grief are playing out within seconds in the mind of the doomed. Up until the time of death when the brain – playing tricks of kindness in the form of hallucinations – reaches acceptance. I think about that whenever I gaze at the painting.

Sometimes I feel sorry that only the privileged few will see this incredible Rembrandt from now on. It's only on display for the eyes of those with cash and connections.

"Hey, Hawkeye." It's my supervisor. "What's up today?"

"Two tours, and a dinner viewing," I say.

In addition to our underground labyrinth of chambers – containing oils to ancient sculptures, Egyptian sarcophagi to Hollywood movie costumes – we have an incredible private restaurant which seats only two at a time. We employ the best, and most discrete, French chef and wait staff. While our clientele consists mostly of political figures, religious leaders and folks so rich their billions cannot be counted, on occasion we do have in the odd actor or musician. I'm told John and Yoko had dinner here, back in my dad's day.

My supervisor nods, and bids me a farewell.

Like most, I find my job boring. It's an important job – one I don't take lightly – but I watch the clock, just like anyone else. I play around on Facebook, I see what's up on Vine. I Tweet. I've got 856 followers on Twitter, under yet another pseudonym. Or would that be a nom de guerre? After all, I am a writer of fiction on Twitter.

I may be bored most of the time but at least my office is nice. It's small, but neat as the proverbial pin and is decorated retro-style with streamlined Art

Deco pieces swiped from various homes and antique shops in Paris. I have no art on the walls – there's enough of that everywhere else in my life.

I've wasted enough time, had some more coffee. I guess now I should get to work. I need to let the chef – we call him Frenchie, and he doesn't seem to mind – know what tonight's anonymous art appreciator and her date will be having for dinner. We don't offer a menu. The client tells us what they want, and we get it. Or more rightly, we steal it.

Nothing here is bought. We have the lowest overhead and maximum profits. That's all I know, though. In the scheme of things, I'm a peon. I am well aware there will be consequences if I ever stray and I am well-paid, so I don't ask questions. I have a whole other life outside these walls.

I press the button on my intercom. "Frenchie, it's Hawkeye."

He answers instantly. His heavily accented, deep voice sounds obsequious, but I detect disdain. I've never actually seen his face but I picture it sharp, hatchet-like.

"Tonight we'll have two guests at 11:30PM. They want Kobe-beef burgers, medium-rare. Please be sure and put all of the condiments on the side. Buns should be lightly toasted. Extra well-done sweet potato fries for him, fresh fruit for her. Please be sure it's not too ripe. No pith. They want two bottles of Krug Clos d'Ambonnay, and for dessert – champagne cupcakes made from the same."

"Got eet," he says. "Bonsoir." He clicks off before I can say goodbye.

I tweet: *Some people think just because they have a French accent, they're better than everyone else.* Then I delete it. Ah, the agony of detweet!

I click a few keys on my computer, and before long it's time for my first client of the night. This gentleman – I call him "Shoes" in my mind because I don't know his real name and he always wears chichi Italian leather loafers with tassels – has been a regular patron for years.

Shoes likes to look at the Medieval artifacts room. There are illuminated manuscripts, suits of armor, jewelry, weaponry, and several panes of stained glass filched from various cathedrals and mausoleums. My favorite Medieval relics are the skeletons, taken by grave-robbers. One of the disembodied skulls is rumored to be the remains of Matilda of Flanders.

Shoes arrives on the dot, his blindfold recently removed, a world-weary smile on his wan, pale face. We nod to each other, but don't speak. I lead him to his favorite chamber, opening the steel pocket door with my eye. The scanner does its thing, and in we go. The armed guards are already inside, of course.

In spite of their presence, I'm not to leave Shoes alone. Not that we don't trust him – quite the contrary. I'm here to be at his beck and call. He sits on the hard, unyielding throne of swords, and stares for a long time at a painting I consider quite amateurish. I stand silently by the door, waiting until he is finished.

Finally, *I* am finished for the day. Nothing special happened, and I'm eager to get back to my personal life.

Stage Two: *Denial*

Badfinger has to be one of the most depressing, and depressed, bands of all time. They were hailed as the "next Beatles" back in the early 1970s but thanks to sad romances, bad breaks and even worse management, they wound up penniless and not one, but two of them dead by their own hands. Hands that once wrote lyrics and played the most beautiful, poignant music did the devil's work and ended their lives.

Badfinger had some plucky pop tunes, such as *Come and Get It* and *No Matter What* but my favorites are the ones about their doomed relationships. *Baby Blue* is a song the lead singer Pete Ham wrote for the love of his life, Dixie Armstrong. It's about how the roving rocker's neglect brought about their breakup, and how he "got what he deserved" when she wouldn't take him back.

Without You is the saddest song, ever. "I can't give... I can't live anymore... without you."

Badfinger seemed poised for success from the start. They opened for top acts like The Yardbirds and The Moody Blues before being signed to The Beatles' Apple Records in 1968. Paul McCartney himself wrote their biggest hit.

But Apple Records was mismanaged, at best.

In 1975, just three days before his 28th birthday, lead singer Pete Ham hanged himself in the garage of his new home in Surrey. On his arms, he left cigarette burns. In his pocket, he left a note blaming Badfinger's manager Stan Polley, calling him a "soulless bastard."

He assured his pregnant girlfriend Anne Herriott he loved her, but "It's better this way." Alone, Anne gave birth to their daughter one month later.

Eight years after that, in 1983, Ham's main songwriting partner Pete Evans also committed suicide by hanging. He used a willow tree in his backyard. This was following disputes over Badfinger's royalties. Too bad he couldn't have... if my gallows humor can be pardoned... hung on until 1994. Mariah Carey had a huge hit with *Without You* and Evans would have made bank.

Maybe money is the root of all evil, I think as I hand the cashier a crisp $20 bill and get only $8.00 back. Parking is highway robbery at the Hollywood & Highland complex. I was there longer than I meant to be, but still.

I now have a mere 45 minutes to get over the hill into the Valley. Highland Avenue crawls, until I finally get to the Cahuenga Pass. I avoid the freeway at this hour... Hell, at almost any hour.

I crank *Suicide Solution*, one of my favorite songs. It's by Ozzy Osbourne, and it was released before I was born. "Suicide is slow with alcohol..."

I hope I won't be late for my group.

We meet in Toluca Lake every Wednesday. As with nearly everything else in my life, it's anonymous. Until it gets personal... but that's another story.

I pull my new, paper-plated Mercedes-Benz SLS AMG Black Series over to a side street and walk a few blocks to the modest, nondescript community center. I don't want anyone in my group to feel bad, don't want them to think I'm better off than them. Don't want to be resented. I'm one of them, after all.

Just a human being, with all the failings and foibles that go along with it.

Some of us have been in the group long enough to be considered OK to be sponsors. I'm a sponsor, but not all the time. For months on end, I just listen and sometimes I share my story. There's no pressure.

Our group is called "Above the Influence." ATI for short.

We have eight right now. James, a real sad sack if ever I saw one, joined about three weeks ago. He hasn't said much, and I'm eager to know more.

One of our newest members is Donna. At least, that's what she calls herself. Whether it's true or not is anybody's guess. Donna suits her, though. She's pretty, and I think that what the name means, though it translates as 'lady' in Italian.

In some ways, she reminds me of my sister.

* * *

When Jessie and me were kids, it was us against the world.

Dad worked all night, every night. He was in the museum of course, though we didn't know it then. We imagined all kinds of cool, clandestine careers for him. Was he an international spy? Maybe he was a pimp-slash-mortician like in our favorite movie, *Night Shift*.

Mom was an alcoholic. That was a full-time job for her, and she took it seriously.

One morning when she was in her room behind a closed door, blackout shades over the windows, I got Jessie ready for school. Same as always, I got the mini stepladder from the side of the fridge and got the cereal down from its dusty top. We liked Life. The cereal, I mean. Life in general was... well, it was all we knew. I was eight, Jessie was six. She was a sweet kid, curious and a little wistful. Unlike mine, her hair was blonde. Her eyes were pale blue. Later they'd remind me of a song by The Velvet Underground. "Linger on, your pale blue eyes..."

She was a good girl, always did what I told her. I rather liked my position of authority. "Drink your juice," I'd command, even as she was doing just that.

We were still in our PJ's that morning. She wore a Cabbage Patch nightie, as I recall. It was early, but our daddy would be home soon. He'd ruffle our hair, then go into the den and turn on the news. Though he slept most of it away anyhow, he liked to be informed what the day's weather would bring. Who knows what he did after Jessie and I went to school.

But Dad wasn't home yet. It was just us.

And Mom.

We had to be very quiet in the mornings. Even at our tender ages, we knew what a hangover was. To us, she was like a sleeping lion. A mane of matted blonde hair (she usually hit the pillow with spray-saturated strands), a nude-colored slip (I could see right through it, and she never wore panties), and a nasty temper (don't even think it). That was Mom.

I say "was" – though I assume she's still alive out there somewhere.

Jessie's not alive anymore. But she was, that morning. She probably wished she wasn't, or at least wished she were invisible. That's what I excelled at: keeping under the radar. Maybe that's why I'm so good at my job today.

Jessie was bouncing around in her chair a bit, as six year old girls will. I'd finished my breakfast and I was in our room, getting dressed. I picked out a blue unicorn tee-shirt and some jeans and flip-flops for my sister to wear, and I was just about to look at the clock when I heard an awful clatter.

Mom and I made it to the kitchen right around the same time, but she got to Jessie first. Jessie had dropped her bowl, and it lay broken on the floor. A few soggy pieces of cereal lay amongst chips and shards of ceramic.

I stood in the open arch between the kitchen and the den. My bare feet straddled the carpeting and linoleum. I said nothing, but I looked at my little sister in mute sympathy.

Mom's stiff Aqua Net coif conflicted texturally with her soft pink peignoir, just as her smooth, fleshy fingertips clashed with her long, sharp nails. She grabbed Jessie by her left upper-arm, and I could picture the bruises and crescent-shaped marks that would be left. If we got to school at all, Jessie would be wearing long sleeves.

Her small body was flung to the floor, her head narrowly missing a table-leg.

Mom pushed the back of Jessie's head to floor by her broken bowl. "See what you did?"

Jessie was silent, but tears flowed down her reddening cheeks.

"Do you think we're made of money? Do you think we can just break dishes and waste food?" She paused, as if waiting for an answer. "Eat it."

Jessie shot me a look. I was helpless. Motionless. Eight years old.

She cast a watery glance up at our mother. *Really?*

Mom nodded, her face set, features fixed in fury.

Jessie picked at a lump of sodden Life, one without any ceramic dust, and did as she was told. There were about five or six pieces in all, some with shards and those had to be eaten too. How she survived that incident relatively unscathed, I'll never know. She didn't have to eat much glass, but even not much is more than enough. I guess stomach acid really is that strong.

She was forced to mop the floor and then piece together the bowl with Krazy Glue. For at least a week, that was Jessie's bowl. After that, Dad must've thrown it away because it just disappeared. I don't know if he ever knew what happened that morning, and I never asked. Such was the way of our household. Don't ask. Don't tell. Be quiet. Keep secrets.

I was fine with that.

But Jessie didn't fare so well. She was always happy, playful, boisterous and bouncy as a baby and a youngster, but over the years she changed. She became bookish, lonesome, and desperate for affection. She stayed with friends as much as she could, proposing slumber parties at their houses, inviting herself over for dinners, to movies and even church on Sundays. Anything to get away.

Maybe that's why Donna reminds me of Jessie. She's talking to another woman in the group. Though she obviously doesn't know this person, she's proposing coffee after the meeting. As if she doesn't want to go home.

Since most of us are regulars, we don't rehash our life stories. This isn't AA, where everyone's labeled an "addict" and made to stand before all those eyes and say, "My name is so-and-so, and I'm an alcoholic."

I did go to Al-Anon for a minute, back when I was 20 or so, but it wasn't for me. I'm not the one with a problem.

I'm above the influence.

Stage Three: *Anger*

I wasn't born yet when Sid Vicious of The Sex Pistols OD'ed on heroin while he awaited trial for the murder of his girlfriend, Nancy Spungen. He killed her in Manhattan's Chelsea Hotel – the same place Leonard Cohen and Bob Dylan wrote poignant love songs to Janis Joplin and Sara Lownds.

On the morning of October 12th in 1978, Sid claimed to have awoken from a drug-dream to find Nancy's lifeless body on the bathroom floor of their room.

She was a junk-whore and an ex-hooker, so I guess it's not surprising she came to a bad end. And it's not surprising Courtney Love wanted to play Nancy in the film version… Both were toxic sirens, as far as I'm concerned.

Nancy suffered a single stab wound to her belly and bled out. The fancy blade had recently been bought by Sid on 42nd Street and was identical to a collector's knife given to his friend Stiv Bators of the Dead Boys by Dee Dee Ramone.

Upon his arrest Sid admitted he'd fought with Nancy, but that she fell on the knife by accident.

Then he said, "I stabbed her, but I didn't mean to kill her."

Ten days later, he tried to slit his wrist with a broken light-bulb. After that he went to Riker's, made bail, and went home with his new girlfriend.

But he never forgot Nancy.

Sid succeeded in his second attempt, this time with powerful heroin supplied by his own mother. Seems like not a bad way to go. Better than a bullet to the brain or hanging yourself, anyway. I've never tried heroin, but I hear it's like the afterglow of an orgasm multiplied by ten. No wonder it's so addictive.

Sid's mom later found a note referencing his slain love, saying, "We had a death pact, and I have to keep my half of the bargain. Please bury me next to my baby. Bury me in my leather jacket, jeans and motorcycle boots. Goodbye."

Adding insult to the ultimate injury, he was cremated and since Nancy was laid to rest in a consecrated Jewish cemetery, Sid's remains could be left nowhere near her.

Right now, I'm near Donna. She's in week two of recovery. She seems fine to everyone else, I'm sure – but I see the fragility. I'm close enough to see the slight blue tint of the vein in her temple, to smell the faint sweetness of her herbal shampoo. Her nails are filed short and rounded (but I see some rough edges), and she wears a faded black sundress.

I'm still curious about James, too. I watch him as he shares his story.

"Afterward, I felt like such a failure," he's saying. His thinning beige hair is slicked back, the length tucked behind his ears. He wears an Ed Hardy tee-shirt – *There's your failure right there*, I think – and whiskered dark wash denim jeans. Cowboy boots, too new.

"I couldn't tell anyone about it, of course. I had to carry on, to present a face to the world of happiness and calm. Of being in control." According to him, it affected his work, his social life. It was all he could think about. Not an uncommon story. His wife, now an ex, knew about it and she made sure he was never alone. She tried to keep him distracted, tried to tell him he was better than that. She got rid of all the bottles.

It didn't work. He wound up in the hospital, and then an asylum of sorts. Rock bottom, but not the end. And here he was, trying to sort it all out. We all offer words on encouragement, pats on the back and clichés. *It's always darkest before the dawn, don't worry it gets better, tough times never last but tough people do.* And so on.

After our meeting, Donna and I go for coffee. She's not ready to talk yet about what's brought her to us, and that's fine. She admires my ring, and I tell her it belonged to my little sister Jessie. I wear it on a chain around my neck. It's my only jewelry, apart from my wedding band. I allude to the fact that Jessie's dead, but Donna doesn't pry.

We talk about mundane things.

"Where are you from?" she asks me. She's enjoying a Grande quad nonfat one-pump no-whip mocha, while I stir at my flavorless, colorless green tea. I'm trying to get on the antioxidant bandwagon, but it's a hard row to hoe. At least tea is gluten-free, so I've got that.

"Here," I say. "I know, I know. Nobody's born and raised in L.A."

"Meet your match," she says.

"No shit? Where from?"

"Temecula. You've probably never heard of it. Maybe that's what drove me to drink," she chuckles.

So she doesn't want to talk, but she wants to hint. I just nod, and sip.

"You don't look like... er..." she falters.

"Oh, I'm not," I say a bit too quickly. "I mean, yeah. I get it. Been there. But nowadays, I counsel. I'm a sponsor. You know, people call me when they're feeling weak." I change the subject. "What's your line of work?"

"I'm not working now. I lost my job."

Oops. I should have known better than to have asked that. I'll avoid romance, family, and pets while I'm at it. "Do you like art?" I ask.

She nods. Who's going to say no to that question? Nobody wants to think themself a philistine.

"There's a great exhibit at LACMA," I say. "It's a retrospective of Llyn Foulkes. Portraiture, narrative tableaux. Existential landscapes, his postwar abstractions."

She blinks, blank.

Tone it down. "His later works focus mainly on Disney. There's some freaky stuff, like Mickey Mouse clawing his way out of Walt's eye."

Donna's right eyebrow shoots up. I just can't seem to get it together, conversationally, today. I smile, and shrug.

"So, you're an expert, are you?" she asks. "Really, all I know is what's popular."

"I know a lot about art. My dad worked in a museum. But I'm no expert. I'd really rather get a mani-pedi and binge-watch Netflix than go to LACMA."

Donna chuckles. "Me, too!" Then the smile disappears. "But I can't afford it these days." She holds out her hands, so I can see her ragged, unpolished fingernails.

"Come on, then. It's on me," I say, trashing my tea in the nearby wastebasket.

"Oh, I don't know," she demurs. I can tell she doesn't want to owe me anything, or maybe doesn't consider herself worthy of a treat on someone she barely knows.

"I insist," I say.

She nods and stands. She's malleable.

There's a chic salon nearby, but I don't want to overwhelm her. I want her to trust me. After all, it's why I do what I do. It's why I've been going to ATI for so many months. I want to help.

There's a place I know a few blocks down the road. I say I'll meet her there, and after parking my car out of sight and changing into the pair of flip-flops I keep in the trunk, I walk over. She's there, having just arrived. Her fingernails are chewed to the nubs, so she opts for the pedi only.

I get scrubbed and buffed. No polish for me, not even clear – though it's offered. No one who works at the museum is allowed to wear anything that might damage a painting or a statue… the swipe of a red fingernail, or a keychain hanging from one's hip, could do disaster. I'm surprised we're not obliged to wear hairnets.

Donna and I chat a little more. I find out she was an only child. That her father was an alcoholic. That she's never been married. That she used to be a bookkeeper. She likes classic literature.

Afterwards, we part ways. We'll see each other in group next week. Maybe I'll tell my story. It's been awhile. What should I say? The possibilities gallop through my mind like so many roughshod horses.

But now it's time to go home and await my chariot to work.

Stage Four: *Bargaining*

WOW. Or Wendy O. Williams as she was better known, was the lead singer of the seminal heavy punk band, The Plasmatics. They reigned from 1978 to '88.

The brash blonde bombshell was known for destruction. She reveled in it. Onstage, she would use sledgehammers or chainsaws to wreak havoc on TV sets, guitars, and Cadillac Coupe de Villes. When she was dressed, she favored nurse outfits, leopard print and black electrical tape over her nipples. Her hair was usually worn in a Mohawk and when she pranced onstage, she channeled a Roman warhorse with a roached mane and fire flowing from its flared nostrils.

She would have liked that analogy, I think. Wendy loved animals. She lived in a dome in the forest, and she spent her final days nursing injured baby squirrels back to life. She was a vegetarian. And an advocate of healthy living...

...That is, when she wasn't trying to kill herself.

In 1993, she stabbed herself in the chest. Actually, she used a hammer to lodge the blade into her sternum. In 1997 she overdosed on ephedrine. But it wasn't until she took a shotgun into the woods, put it to her head and pulled the trigger, that she succeeded in her grim goal.

Wendy was a thoughtful suicide. She set aside presents for her longtime love, Rod Swenson, including his favorite noodles, seeds for salad greens, and oriental massage balm. She left a note: "My feelings about what I am doing ring loud and clear to an inner ear and a place where there is no self, only calm."

She wanted to die. Maybe that's why she sings with such fierce conviction on *It's My Life*, a song written by Gene Simmons and Paul Stanley of KISS, and first released on her 1984 album *WOW*. It was her life. Hers to live, hers to take.

If someone decides they want to die, they should be allowed to make it happen.

That's how I've always felt, even before Jessie died.

After Jessie died, I learned what the legal terms were for acts which arose from those feelings. Depraved-heart murder. Reckless endangerment. Culpable negligence. Did you know suicide is illegal? Well, no one attempting suicide has ever been prosecuted, but it's construed as a crime nonetheless, because it allows the state to lawfully detain you for treatment without your consent. But people have been prosecuted for encouraging suicide in others... Say, during a friendly game of Russian Roulette. The winner is really a loser, in the eyes of the law.

But that's a pretty clumsy way of doing it. Getting someone to kill themselves, I mean.

Putting a pistol in a depressed person's quivering hand, that's easy. Or plying the bereaved with booze and downers, putting them in front of the TV and sticking in a DVD of *Angela's Ashes*. That's child's play.

But tipping someone over the edge who doesn't really want to die? That's the rabbit from the hat.

I shouldn't be dwelling on the past. I'll get back to Jessie again, I promise. Right now, I need to think about... now.

It's a big day at work. I have three showings, which is going to show up big on my paycheck.

First, I have a very famous reality TV producer coming in to see – but not touch. No touching allowed. It's the magnificent Davidoff-Morini Stradivarius violin. What a beauty it is! In October 1995, the $3 million 1727 instrument was stolen from renowned violinist Erica Morini's New York apartment. Poor Morini, who was 91 years old, died shortly after the robbery. Perhaps its loss was just too much for her frail soul to bear. But the melody-maker lives on, cloistered within the walls of our magnificent museum.

After that, I have a client flying all the way in from Jordan to see one our Picassos. It's *The Pigeon With Green Peas* (AKA, *Le Pigeon Aux Petits Pois*) and it was snatched from the Musée d'Art Moderne de la Ville de Paris in 2010. The lone thief was later convicted, though he was found empty-handed. The guy said he threw it in the trash, but the framed canvas was never found. And it never will be.

Lastly, I'm showing one of my personal favorites, a religious piece by Jan van Eyck's called *The Just Judges*. (Though some folks suspect his brother, Hubert, might be the actual painter.)

Before my dad was even a gleam in his dad's eye, this trinket was taken from its display at Saint Bavon's Cathedral in Ghent, Belgium, where it served as part of the *Adoration of the Lamb* altarpiece created in the mid-1400s. There were some ransom notes swirling around in the 1930s shortly after it was swiped, and the self-proclaimed thief – a flamboyant politician, artist, and lover of detective novels, named Arsène Goedertier – revealed with his dying breath that only he knew where the painting was hidden, and that he would take the secret with him to his grave.

The Just Judges is the lower left panel of the Ghent Altarpiece, and it shows portraits of several contemporary figures such as Philip the Good, and possibly the artists Hubert and Jan van Eyck themselves. In the forefront is a serene-faced young man astride a magnificent white stallion, its mane – perhaps a bit like Wendy O. Williams' bleached blonde hair – flowing in the winds of change.

I've done lots of research on this one. I must admit, I'm fascinated with what drives people to steal. I'm not talking about Jean Valjean style stealing, a loaf of bread to survive. We can all understand that. Then there's the thrill of taking something of value, something you don't actually need. The plotting, the planning, the devising, and the deft skill.

To steal a thing is a tangible act. People notice. But to steal a life, without detection, now that's real talent.

* * *

"If you'd just stay here and help out, I'll buy you a car," Mom pleaded. "How about a classic Mustang?"

She was always doing that. Bribing us. Making bargains. "If you do this, I'll do that." She made it seem so easy. It never was, of course.

Dad had left us by then. It was just me, Jessie, and our mother. I was 18, and I could have gone out on my own.

But I couldn't leave Jessie with her. Being with Mom felt like being choked from the inside. I figured being *alone* with Mom must've been infinitely worse.

Jessie was almost 16. She'd talked to Dad about it, and he said, "It's up to your mother."

My sister wanted to go away to study. In Paris. She would rather spend her time with brooding, espresso-sipping French intellectuals who seem to do nothing for a living and have all the time in the world to ponder deep philosophical things in Left Bank cafés.

That would not do. She couldn't leave me. I wouldn't allow it.

The idea came to me one night while I was in my bedroom, listening to music. I put on Bad Company's *Shooting Star*. Although Paul Rodgers didn't kill himself (at least, not yet. He's still alive and well as I write this), the lyrics portray an alternate reality the singer envisioned for himself, had he succumbed to the deepest depths of rock 'n roll decadence. "Johnny died one night, died in his bed. Bottle of whiskey, sleeping tablets by his head."

Although she'd cauterized her emotions to the point of nonexistence around others, Jessie was always honest with me. I knew her pain. I knew how to bring it out.

A few years before, I'd talked Jessie into keeping a journal. I told her I kept one too, to hold our secrets and to keep a record of our pain. I didn't, though. Not then. I simply read hers, and soothed my soul with her words. She wrote about the solace of suicide. Sylvia Plath poetry mixed with rock lyrics was vomited onto the thin, cheap pages over and over again, along with the occasional teenager frivolity about cute boys and sexy shoes.

One phrase in Jessie's journal always stuck with me: "Unexpected death is an abduction." I don't know if they were her own words or not, but they made sense.

In the end, there was no bargain. Mom simply said, "No, Jessie. You can't go." And that was the beginning of the end.

Stage Five: *Guilt*

When I think of suicide by shotgun, I think of men. Hard-drinking, hard-riding, hard-handed men. Ernest Hemingway. Hunter S. Thompson. Calluses against metal as they squeezed the grip.

Women usually go for the soft embrace of drugs and alcohol. *Usually.*

Mindy McCready couldn't been any more different, musically, from fellow trigger-puller

Wendy O. Williams. She was an angel-faced country chick, with a sweet smile and a touch of sass. She had a handful of hits, but all too quickly fell from fame's fleeting graces. She spiraled into the usual depression and addictions.

Ironically, just days before she shot herself on her front porch, she was working on a suicide prevention video. Presumably, it was to assuage her own grief and guilt after the front porch shotgun suicide of her boyfriend a month earlier. But later, friends speculated Mindy was actually warning them that she was next.

Too bad nobody warned the family dog. Yep, that's right. The singer popped the pooch just before doing herself in. I always thought that was a strange touch. I mean, what for – to ensure she'd feel bad enough about herself to be able to put the gun to her own head? To test how quick and hopefully painless it would be?

There was some speculation that Mindy actually killed her boyfriend, that his death wasn't a suicide at all.

The couple had a baby son. Talk about tragedy.

In fact, I'm talking about it tonight. It's Wednesday again, and time for another ATI meeting.

I'm going to offer to sponsor Donna. She needs me. I can tell. I want to help her, like I helped Jessie. And Jasmine.

(I'll get to Jasmine, later.)

I stand at the podium, looking out over the wan, deeply shadowed faces, hard-edged in the cheap fluorescent tube-lighting and years of pain, anguish and self-doubt. These are my people. A black-haired, dark-eyed messiah, my nails buffed, teeth gleaming, and dressed in a dark eggplant silk shirt, classic slacks and sandals, I knew I had the admiration – and envy – of them all.

James has just finished sharing. Again. At first, he didn't say much. Now he won't shut the fuck up about his one measly suicide attempt. Of course, I'm all grace and compassion. I beam at him. "James. That was beautiful. And you are so right. There's no time like the present. And there's no present like time. We mustn't waste it."

James, still wearing egregious Ed Hardy, clasps his hands together and juts them out, mouthing, "Thank you."

I glance over at Donna. She catches my eye, then smiles and dips her gaze. She likes me. I can tell.

While everyone else is slurping caffeinated swill from white Styrofoam cups, I've got my Starbucks Thanksgiving blend. (Yeah, I just couldn't do the green tea.) I take a small sip, before beginning. I clear my throat, pretending I'm nervous. I pull Jessie's ring to and fro along the string of platinum chain around my neck. I give a half-smile, a faint chuckle.

"I haven't told my story in a long time. But there are enough new faces here, to warrant a re-telling. It's not easy, even after all these years…"

* * *

The sheets are damp, steamy, and rumpled from our first time together. Donna and me. Her fingertips trace my jawline. The corners of my mouth rise in a smile that follows the smooth, sensuous tickle.

She tilts her head, and looks at me. Somewhere nearby, a weak streetlamp shines stubbornly through the slats of her cheap, white plastic blinds. Her bittersweet chocolate eyes are so dark, they're nearly black.

"Where'd you get that scar?" she asks, touching the thin white line on my chin.

"Handlebars of my Huffy."

"A bike?"

"Yes. But not just any bike. I was a very discerning nine-year-old. I had a genuine vintage Slingshot model with 16" front dragster wheel, and 20" rear. I pimped it out with a Flaming Stack chain guard, which was designed to look just like the side exhaust pipe covers of a Corvette."

"Sounds like you were a bit of daredevil," she smiles.

She takes my left hand in hers. I slipped the wedding band off before getting into bed with her, though of course she's seen it before.

"Yeah. The bike was totaled," I sigh. "But that's nothing compared to this," I say, lowering the sheet a little so she could get a good look at the long, wavy scar just under my right pec.

"Botched boob job?" she jokes.

"Funny. I like that. You're a real card, you know that? An ace." I scruff her hair playfully, then go on. "This is from the bill of a marlin. I was fishing off the coast —"

"Which is way better than fishing on the coast."

"You're a regular comedian, aren't you?" I grin. But really, I am getting a bit miffed at all these interruptions.

"—off the coast in the northern Atlantic. I had the bastard hooked, and it was like something out of a Hemingway novel —"

"*The Old Man and the Sea?*"

"Right. Anyway, the slick S.O.B. comes flying right at me, and grazed me with his nose, which is like a swordfish's. I was bleeding like I'd been gored by a bull —"

"*Death in the Afternoon.*"

I sigh. "You know your Hemingway. Good. OK, so anyway, I'm gushing blood, and this titan is flopping all over the deck. That sword of his is like an out of control chainsaw, and I'm dancing around, trying to avoid getting hamstrung. Finally, I grab a folding chair and start beating this thing over the head until it stops moving."

"Oh, my God. That must have been terrifying!"

"Not really. At the end of the day, he was delicious. I sautéed him in a butter and garlic sauce, with a touch of port. He fed me for a week. All's well that ends well."

She shakes her head.

"I have some scars, too." Donna's gaze dips. She's pensive, now.

She's so pretty. Not a very enthusiastic bedmate, but lovely to look at. Besides, it's only our first time. I'll get her to come around. To want and need me, and only me. This is a very important stage in our relationship. It's about earning trust. She already likes me. I can tell that one day soon, she might even love me. But that's not what I'm after. She has to trust me more than she trusts herself. More than she trusts her own instincts. Like that marlin, I have to hook her before I can cook her. (So to speak. I'm no Jeffrey Dahmer, if that's what you're thinking.)

Anyway, I know the routine. It never fails. Charm, and disarm. Tell her she's gorgeous, smart, funny, great in bed. Whatever it takes. Then, I start chipping away.

As Michelangelo once said, "It's my job to free the human form trapped inside the block." Donna is like a precious work of art. She's like one of the Elgin Marbles. My work begins with the selection of a perfect, yet unformed shape. After I find my stone, one that speaks to me, I begin chiseling. Getting rid of the parts I don't want: self-esteem, the ability to make unilateral decisions, and confidence. Especially confidence. Then I'll place the tapered point of my chisel against a selected part of the stone, swinging the mallet at it with precisely controlled strokes, careful to strike accurately. The smallest miscalculation could damage the stone, not to mention the sculptor's hand.

I take her hands. Gently turn them palms-up. "I know about those scars. Show me another one."

Donna smiles again. Shyly. I can smell the faint mint residue on her teeth, and the musk of my kisses. She moves her right leg out from under the crisp, crumpled sheet. She brings it up, so her knee is held aloft. There's a scar in the folds of flesh.

"My knees are so ugly, you probably can't even see it. But right there," she points, "is where I fell while getting out of the limo at my high school prom."

"Oh, man. Seriously? You fell in front of everyone at your prom?"

"The story of my life," she says, sighing. Then she shrugs.

I can tell the memory still haunts her. She feels things very deeply. They affect her. She doesn't let go.

This is good for me.

* * *

My one regret is that I wasn't there when Jessie killed herself.

I was there for Jasmine. Oh, yes. I made sure of that.

But like I said, the first time isn't always the best. You know you want to do it again, you vow to hone your technique, and sure enough – it gets better.

Jasmine was my fiancée. Ten days before our wedding, she overdosed on pills. I held her in my arms, made sure she kept everything down… I knew she wouldn't want to be found in a puddle of vomit. Besides, what if she'd tossed the lethal cocktail? That would not do.

Now, you might be wondering, if you're fan of morbid primetime true crime, *Why didn't I wait a while? Why not get married, insure her life, and then pull the curtains?* I find that vulgar. Money as a motive. I can make money. Anyone can make money. But to be a honed, undetectable killing machine that never once lays a finger on his prey? To make them think it's their idea? That, my friend, is pure talent.

You have to willing to change things up, shake them up. Not follow any pattern. I like to think I have a jazz brain, and rock 'n roll soul.

I'm like the David Bowie song, *Rock 'n Roll Suicide*. If only the world knew about me, I'd have fist-pumping lighter waving hordes in my wake, wherever I go. "So natural, religiously unkind…"

I learned a lot about Jasmine in the few months she was my patient. Not officially. I'm not a PhD., or a certified therapist or anything like that. But I told Jasmine I was. Told her lots of things. She believed them all. When I told her I loved her and that I would be there for her until the end, she believed me.

One of my favorite ways in – and women love this; they dig psychology – is a little litmus test that goes like this. I take her out to dinner. A nice, but not too nice, romantic hideaway where we have a light dinner and lots of wine. She's loose, happy, and feeling pretty in the candlelight. I hold her hand, placing it in my lap. Nothing too overt, merely suggestive. If she doesn't pull away… and mind you, this is on the third or fourth date… I know I can start chiseling.

I tell a story, asking questions along the way. "You are walking in the woods. It's a beautiful, idyllic place. Who are you walking with?" Whomever she says, that's the most important person in her life. If she says, "No one. I'm alone," that's a great sign for me to move ahead. Next I'll ask, "You see an animal in these woods. What kind of animal is it?" The animal is representative of her perception of the size of her problems. So if she says it's a bunny, then that's not as good for me as if she were to say a grizzly bear or a mountain lion. (Now, if she says "a penguin" or something like that, then I know she's either bat-shit crazy or has no idea what kinds of animals live in the forest.)

Then I tell her she comes to a house, and I ask her to describe it to me. I can get a lot from that, but what I really want to know is, "Is there a fence around this house?" If not, then she hasn't got many walls up and I can get in a little easier. Then I say she goes in, and she sees a table in the kitchen. I ask her to describe the table. If her reply does not include food, people, or flowers, then I know she's secretly unhappy. This is good news. Overtly unhappy people aren't very likely to off themselves. It's the quiet ones you have to watch for.

The test goes on. There's a huge tree felled in the forest and I find out how she gets around it. These represent her problems; so does she climb over the tree? Dig under it? Go around? The best one is about the body of water she comes to. This is how she views love and sex. Is the surface glassy? Can she see clearly into the water? Is it murky? Is it cold, or warm? Does she want to take a swim, or not?

Jasmine answered all these questions just about the same way Jessie did. It's not foolproof, but damn near close.

Jessie was pretty distraught when I gave her the test. She loved answering my questions, though. She thought I was asking because I really cared about her, and wanted to help her. Well, maybe I did. I was younger, then. More idealistic.

I loved Jessie, but I also loved my power over her.

Jessie was almost 17 by now. She was becoming a woman in some ways; physically, anyway. She had that burgeoning bloom of youth, curves appearing where before there were only angles, elbows and knees. Her eyes were clear and bright, but usually downcast either in thought or worry. Mom was a constant source of worry. We both still lived with her in our palace of eggshells and glass.

I didn't tell anyone (not even my sweet sis), but I'd opened up a line of communication with Dad. I knew someday soon, I'd be joining him in his very special line of work. Instead of Jessie leaving me, I'd be leaving her.

Or maybe I could have my marlin, and eat it too.

When Jessie was gone, I'd read her diary. Then I'd carefully put it away, seemingly undisturbed. When we'd later have casual conversations, heart-to-hearts, or even just joking around, I'd throw in little tidbits about her I'd learned from reading the journal. She was amazed at the depth of my perception. How well I knew her. How I was the only one who really, really knew her. Or I'd pose a thought similar to something she'd been thinking. "We are so much alike," she'd marvel. I'd nod in mutual amazement, the picture of perspicuity.

So much alike. After a few months, I began to suggest to her that we were just the same as our mother. No good. Unlovable. We'd never be worthy of a soul-mate. Who in their right minds could ever really care about us? There was something wrong with us. We were fucked up, and that would never change. It was in our blood.

So why bother going on living?

I told Jessie I wanted to kill myself.

She nodded, hugging herself as if wrapped in a placenta of grief and self-loathing. "Me, too."

The last words she wrote in her journal were, "I love you."

Stage Six: *Depression*

Sometimes, you have to find the good in goodbye. And it seems the rakishly handsome, ringlet-haired lothario-like lead singer of the Australian pop band INXS did just that.

Michael Hutchence went out erotically asphyxiated, so maybe he died with a smile on his face. I like to think so. The poor guy deserved that, at least.

In death as in life, his story was front and center of a media circus. Before his nude body was found on the morning of November 22, 1997 by a maid in his Ritz-Carlton Sydney hotel room – #524, booked to a Mr. Murray Rivers – Michael's messy life was splashed across all the rags. He was in torment not only over extreme drug addiction, but because it would be a Christmas without his beloved 16-month-old daughter, Heavenly Hiraani Tiger Lily. Lily's mother, a bottle-blonde TV personality named Paula Yates, was in a bitter custody battle with the father of her other children, Bob Geldof. It was a nightmare all around.

Michael was terribly depressed by most accounts, especially after a freak accident a few years earlier had robbed him of most of his senses of taste and smell. A cocktail of alcohol, cocaine, and Prozac was later noted by the coroner.

Michael hung out with friends, then phoned a few people before meeting his maker. One of his ex-girlfriends was so worried she actually went to his hotel room and knocked on the door on the morning of his death, but he didn't answer. Maybe he was already gone. The last time his voice, that voice which was on so many hit records, was recorded was on his personal manager, Martha Troup's, voicemail. He said, "Marth, Michael here. I've fucking had enough."

Far from "Elegantly Wasted," Michael was pathetic in the end. He didn't die pretty. There was evidence he'd scrounged through wastebaskets, searching for even a crumb of leftover cocaine, and there was a week-old cigarette burn on one of his fingers that had gone down to the bone, indicating he'd passed out and didn't even feel the pain. In the same trash can he'd dumpster-dived for drugs, police later found lyrics to the last song he wrote – which have never been published.

His death was ruled a suicide by auto-erotic asphyxia.

Apparently, this form of sex-play is not uncommon amongst more adventurous paramours. When it's done with a partner, the act is called Breath Control Play. But what it really is, is strangulation without death (hopefully). The carotid arteries on the sides of the neck flow the most oxygen-rich blood to the brain, and so restricting that stream produces lightheadedness and even giddiness, which surges the sensations during sex. When pressure is released, the rush of that elemental necessity to the brain is a *zing!* of pure euphoria.

When engaged in a little hand-to-gland combat, the soloist can use a plastic bag over the head, or a belt or scarf around his neck.

Michael Hutchence opted for a snakeskin belt. Three years later, Paula Yates opted for heroin, leaving Lily to grow up without her parents.

* * *

Jessie and me grew up without parents. Real, normal, present ones, anyway. I only got close to my dad later, after Jessie's suicide. And following her funeral, Mom disappeared altogether. Good riddance, I say.

I'd told Jasmine about most of this, tailored to fit my needs of course, shortly after we met. I think it made her trust me that much more as her therapist and her confidant. She thought I got it. Got *her*. Poor, trusting Jasmine.

We never did live together or exchange house keys. My work schedule wasn't known to her, only my limited availability. At first, she assumed I was married and not hiding it too well. I talked her out of that nonsense, leaving out the fact I was divorced. From a man. Does that make me a widow, or a widower? I always get the two mixed up. In any case, I'm far too evolved to be defined by something as base as gender. I'm beyond all that. Divine.

No, I'm not delusional. I know I'm just a little-ol' flesh and bone human being. Some might say I'm like a surgeon with a God complex. Nothing could be further from the truth. Just because I've used psychological shenanigans on others doesn't mean I'm blind to my own... well, I wouldn't call them *faults*. More like, peculiarities. Yes, I like that: I'm "peculiar."

In case you're wondering why no-one's connected all these deadly dots, it's because I'm a well-kept secret. All of us who work within the walls of the museum are provided with a brand-new identity every six months like Swiss clockwork.

Anyway, it was a moonless Wednesday night when Jasmine faded from this world. I'll never forget it. It was truly transcendental.

I told her it was the right thing to do. Everyone would, indeed, be better off without her. "No one will miss you, Jasmine," I said softly. Her entire existence was nothing but a cacophony of monotony. Pointless. Futile. *End it now, before it gets too painful.* I put on some soothing music, poured her a glass of rich red wine, and gave her a handful of pills, which she accepted gratefully. She really did. "Thank you," she said breathily between swallows.

The room was candle-lit, the aroma was of warm sandalwood.

I held her until she was no more. I watched her blue eyes, nearly the same shade as Jessie's, close for the last time. There was no violence. No sickness. No fight.

Nothing but ragdoll limbs and a lolling head as I dragged her slight form off the bed and slipped her inside the waiting bath. With her final, shallow breath, she inhaled oil-slick, soapy water and cinched the coroner's report of accidental suicide by drowning.

* * *

I've just been dropped off at the museum. I walk to the front entrance of LACMA, where the *Urban Lamps* light my way. Standing in the middle of the metallic forest, I flick that familiar, flush switch. Without a sound I'm lowered underground by the high-tech trapdoor.

I nod and smile at Lefty. She smiles curtly back, mouth-corners raised, no teeth showing. Tonight she's dressed in a Chinese dress – a cheongsam. It's red, with gold dragons on it. We're sort of in synch. Even though I'm in slate grey, my scarf is scarlet with flecks of gilt.

I pass *Hannibal.* I go through the Dutch corridor and I pause to admire Vermeer's *The Concert.* I linger at *Storm on the Sea of Galilee.*

And now, I'm in my office looking over the night's assignments. One of my favorites – a client we call "The Encyclopedia" because he reels off facts at the speed of light (which is approximately 186,000 miles per second, he once told me) – will be here in an hour (3,600 seconds).

Encyclopedia wants to see the famous Ruby Slippers from the classic 1939 film, *The Wizard of Oz.* Mind you, these aren't the only pair ever made. And they're not even worth all that much – only about $2 million. But we have lots of movie memorabilia. It's a popular display in this town.

This particular pair of kicks disappeared on August 27, 2005, from the Judy Garland Museum in Grand Rapids, Minnesota. No one's tried clicking the heels together three times to see if they'll find their way home, but I can't say I haven't been tempted.

They sparkle prettily under the spotlight. So small and delicate. Not many people know this, but Dorothy's supernatural shoes were actually described as silver slippers in the 1900 novel written by L. Frank Baum. MGM's costume designer Gilbert Adrian decided to switch the hue in order to take advantage of the gorgeous glitter effect on the sequined slippers when it was decided the movie would be shot using the brand-new three-strip Technicolor film process.

The bell dings, and I head for the door to the vault. Lefty is there, with Encyclopedia. His blindfold has been removed, and his hair is a bit mussed. Otherwise, he's the picture of perfection: shined shoes, creased slacks, starched shirt, silk tie.

"Thank you," I nod a dismiss to Lefty. She disappears down the corridor.

I move forward, shake Encyclopedia's hand heartily, and smile big. "Welcome back! It is so good to see you again, sir."

"Likewise," he replies, stepping into the room. His eyes go immediately to the gleaming ruby slippers.

I lead the way, and we stop at the Plexiglas podium on which they sit.

"Gorgeous! Just magnificent," he says reverently.

"Indeed."

Still staring at the shoes, he asks, "How many times have you seen *The Wizard of Oz*?"

I shrug. "A dozen? It was on TV every Easter when I was young. I guess nowadays a kid can see it anytime."

He sighs. "Yes. Instant gratification. No anticipation." He pauses, glances at me. "Ever watch it again, as an adult?"

"Only if you count the whole 'Dark Side of the Rainbow' thing," I say with an impish grin.

His brows raise. "Hm?"

I tilt my head. "You mean... you don't know...?"

He shrugs.

"Well, if you start playing the movie at the third MGM lion-roar and begin Pink Floyd's *Dark Side of the Moon* album at precisely that moment, here's what happens: when you hear the lyrics 'The lunatic is on the grass' you'll see the Scarecrow dancing on a lawn. Then when the Scarecrow and Dorothy start skipping down the yellow brick road, you'll hear 'Got to keep the loonies on the path.' And when the lyrics 'Don't give me that do goody-goody bull' come on, that's when Glenda the Good Witch ascends in her magic bubble. When the song *Brain Damage* starts? Well, that's when the Scarecrow launches into his 'If I only had a brain' lament. And so on."

"Wow," Encyclopedia says. "I'm impressed."

"Oh, there's more. You should try it sometime. Cannabis helps."

He chuckles. Not to be outdone, he quizzes me. "Did you know that Toto the dog was actually a girl? Her name was Terry, and she was a Cairn Terrier. Before costarring with Judy Garland, she was in a movie with Shirley Temple called *Bright Eyes*. She went on to have puppies who were also in pictures."

I nod, already formulating my response. We have this little one-upmanship thing going on. He loves it. I am sure of this, otherwise I'd never do it. Our clients and their satisfaction is our utmost priority. "Speaking of dogs," I say, "The Beatles song *A Day in the Life* has an extra high-pitched whistle in it, audible only to canines. It was slipped in there by Paul McCartney especially for his Shetland Sheepdog."

"Really? What was the dog's name?"

Uh-oh. "I don't know."

He smiles, smug. "Martha. In fact, he wrote a song about her, called *Martha, My Dear.*"

"Hm." I think for a moment. "OK, well, did you know Robert Plant, the lead singer of Led Zeppelin, wrote a song for his favorite dog, too?"

"Yes. *Black Dog.*"

"Nope." I had him now.

Encyclopedia was stumped.

"The song is called *Bron-Y-Aur Stomp*," I say, praying I'm pronouncing the Welsh correctly, "and it's about his blue-eyed Merle, Strider."

"Named after the *Lord of the Rings* character?"

I nod. Jeez. I never can stay ahead of Encyclopedia for very long. I give up. "Would you like a glass of champagne, sir? Or perhaps an Australian sparkling red?"

He nods. "The red. Of course," a wink. "Thank you."

I shoot a text to Lefty, who in turn makes it happen. Moments later, a valet appears with a cut-crystal goblet of ruby-red wine on a silver tray.

I take a seat nearby, letting Encyclopedia roam the display on his own. I open my Twitter app, and I post a quote by T.S. Eliot. "Only those who will risk going too far can possibly find out how far one can go."

My thoughts wander to Donna, and my plans. I want to try something different this time. Up the stakes. Take a risk.

Stage Seven: *Acceptance*

"Joy Division" was a term coined by the Nazis. It's a euphemism for the sadistic, sexual assaults perpetrated by the SS on their young female prisoners.

Then there's the British post-punk, new wave electronica band called Joy Division. Lead singer and lyricist Ian Curtis and his bandmates Stephen Morris, Peter Hook and Bernard Sumner decided on that name because their fathers had all fought in World War II. That's the reason they called themselves Joy Division, not the glorification of rape. Or so they say.

Ian had accepted for a long time that he would die. If not sooner, than later. But why prolong the inevitable? You see, he had terrible blackouts brought on by epilepsy. More than once, he'd had them onstage while performing. Some audience members thought it was part of the show, but Ian was mortified. He spiraled into depression. Although they were becoming ever more popular, the band never did make it overseas for their first-ever U.S. tour. Their single, *Love Will Tear Us Apart* was a hit, and every hip kid in America wanted to see them.

On May 18, 1980, Ian was home alone. He watched the Werner Herzog film, *Stroszek*, released in 1977. I looked it up, because I've never seen it. One contemporary review says, "For all the supposed lightness, it is the film's core of despair which in the end devours everything." Apparently – spoiler alert – the hero of the story, a Berlin street performer who makes the trek to Middle America, dies of self-immolation on a ski-lift. I, of all people, believe in the power of suggestion. Seeing this must have pushed 23-year-old Ian over the edge.

He didn't set himself ablaze, though. Ian opted, like so many others before him, for hanging. Why is it that singers, whose voice rises from their diaphragm, lungs, and vocal chords, choose the method of strangulation in which to forever silence themselves?

While an Iggy Pop album played, Ian wrote a long letter to his estranged wife, Deborah. He knew she'd be home in a few hours, where she'd find it — and him. Romantic, or cruel? I can't decide.

The despondent singer got a laundry line, and in his kitchen he ended it all. If he was like most home-hangers, then he didn't have a long enough drop to break his neck and go instantly. He probably felt instinctive panic for a few moments before losing consciousness, then finally slipped away.

Ian was, like the film character Bruno Stroszek, put to fire a few days later. Cremated. Deborah Curtis had the words "Love Will Tear Us Apart" inscribed on his tombstone.

* * *

In late June of 2008, someone stole the stone marker. It's never been recovered.

That's because it's at the museum, along with Jim Morrison's funereal bust, and Edgar Allen Poe's bronze effigy which was swiped back in the 70s. We have a special place called The Chamber of Curses. You would not believe the wait list, but as with all of our exhibits, each client gets complete privacy. On only very rare occasions are plus-ones allowed.

I'm especially fond of The Chamber of Curses, because I'm the curator. A morbid magpie, I've collected the best of the dead. In this room, which is painted a bright, happy yellow and boasts a mural of hand-painted bluebells, we have not only stolen stones and monuments, but famous murder weapons, burial clothes and yes, even body parts. Poet Percy Shelley's heart. Mad monk Rasputin's mummified, thirteen-inch member (the one floating in formaldehyde at the Russian Museum of Erotica ain't it). A lock of murderess Lizzie Borden's hair. Her ax. OJ Simpson's knife. And my personal favorite, the icepick used to lobotomize famous 1940s actress Frances Farmer.

Sometimes, I fantasize about driving it up through my eye, and into my brain. I once watched an old PBS documentary clip on YouTube, about Walter Jackson Freeman, the American physician who invented the transorbital lobotomy. He used icepicks from his own kitchen, and the tap-tap of a mallet. It doesn't look painful, and it erases all the bad memories.

But enough about me. Tonight, it's all about Donna. Not the end game, of course. Not yet. That could take months, maybe even a year or more. But I am going to add the new ingredient. It's dangerous, but exciting.

I'm taking her out to a nice, but not intimidatingly expensive, restaurant. Pace (pronounced "pa-chey") on Laurel Canyon Boulevard, just steps from the famous "Love Street" immortalized on an album by The Doors, is upscale but cozy. Brick and ivy, recessed dining room. They have the best pizza in L.A., and even better spirits. We'll sit out in the covered patio, just below ground level, and whisper sweet everythings by candlelight.

I'll tell her more about me than anyone has ever known. Is forewarned forearmed, or will she be a self-fulfilling prophecy?

* * *

"I still think about it sometimes," Donna admits, matter-of-factly. "How I'll do it. When. Why." She nibbles at the dry crust of her pizza slice, as if to stop herself from saying more.

I nod. "Yes. It never goes away."

"That's not very positive, coming from you. My sponsor." She seems more curious, than anything. "Have you ever, um… lost someone in recovery?"

My sigh is heavy. It says *yes* without the word.

"Oh, my god. I'm sorry. I shouldn't have asked."

I hold up a hand. "No, no. Nothing is off-limits. Ask me anything." Inwardly, I'm beaming. She's playing right into it.

She's got her hair pulled back tonight, into a loose chignon. Her lips are tinted nude, bringing out the darkness of her eyes. Her eyes are almonds of depth and intellect, and usually a bit sad. Right now, they're searching mine.

My eyes are dark, too. And piercing. That's why my codename at work is Hawkeye. It's really who I am. Like a bird of prey, I can spot fresh meat from the greatest of great distances. But I'm not ready to swoop in just yet.

Donna looks at the flickering flame, fragile as a life. One quick blow, or a slow burn to the wick – either way, it's inevitably extinguished. She chuckles a little nervously. "That's OK. I really don't want to talk about it tonight. Let's have a good time."

"We are," I say, reaching across the table to take her hand. Her fingertips are finely dusted with pizza crust flour.

She gives a gentle squeeze. "Yes. A good time." She pauses. "I have something to tell you."

"What?"

She looks down, then meets my gaze. "I love you."

I gasp. Not from surprise at her declaration. I expected that. It was her eyes. Her pale, blue eyes.

I blink, and look at her again. Her eyes are brown as ever.

My surprise, and long pause, unsettle her.

"I'm sorry," she mutters, withdrawing her hand from mine. "I shouldn't have said that."

I collect my wits. "Donna. Please, it's not that. I love you, too."

"You're just saying that now. I'm so embarrassed."

But I do love her. Or at least, what she could be. Mine. Soul and body, mine. I take her hand again. "I'm not. Really. It's just," I grin, impishly. "You stole my thunder. That's why I brought you here tonight. Plied you with pizza and white wine…"

We laugh. But it's awkward.

And that's good. I have her a little off-balance. A little unsure of herself. Of me.

Problem is: I'm unsure of myself, too.

I refill her flute, then mine. Almost to the rim. I drink it in two long swallows, then pour more. I'm surreptitiously searching her eyes. Her dark *brown* eyes.

I shudder. *What just happened?*

* * *

We made love that night after dinner. I kept my eyes closed for most of it, telling myself it was merely to heighten my other senses. I slept, but fitfully. I dreamed in shades of cobalt.

It's a couple of days later, and I'm better now. It must have been the wine. Fatigue. Mercury in retrograde. Could have been anything.

Donna and I are sitting in her kitchen sipping hot, black coffee. I've added a pinch of cinnamon to mine. It's still powdery laying on the surface, and its dryness makes me cough a bit. But it tastes sweet.

Now is as good a time as any. "Donna," I begin. "I haven't been telling the whole truth at the ATI meetings."

She nods, once. "I'm sure everyone holds something back. It's just too painful. And private…"

"No. I mean: I've never tried to kill myself."

Her eyes widen. Her mouth doesn't exactly fall open, but her lips part. "What are you saying?" She leaps to the worst possible conclusion immediately. "Are you some kind of grief groupie? I've heard about people who —"

I hold my hands up. Defensive. "It's not like that."

She puts her mug down on the tile counter. I see age-old dirt in the grout, and wonder why grout is always white. She's waiting for my reply.

I take my time. I want her to get a little angry, work it up, so she will feel that much more guilty about thinking so poorly of me.

I let out an audible breath. "My little sister killed herself."

"Go on…" she prompts, probably wondering why I'm not in the appropriate support group. Seeking closure, commiserating, crying, the whole bit.

"I'm not in ATI to trick anyone…"

"But you lied to us! To *me*. I thought you really understood me…" She shrinks, and hugs herself.

"I do. I understand you better than you understand yourself." Maintain the upper hand. Keep sowing the seeds of self-doubt. That I know more than she does. I shrug. "Oh, never mind. I don't know why I even thought I could confide in you. You're not special, you're just like all the rest."

This clearly stings. "No, I'm not. I want to hear. I'm sorry. I'm really sorry. Come on, honey. Tell me," she begs.

I make a show of relenting. I sit up straight at the breakfast nook and spread my arms out, owning the space.

"Her name was Jessie. She was two years younger than me. She was 17 when she did it… and to this day, I have no idea why." I swallow. "I couldn't save her."

Donna sidles over to me. I can feel her warmth. "You were a kid yourself. It's not your fault."

"She hung herself," I say softly, pulling her ring to-and-fro across the chain around my neck. "I found her."

"Oh, God. You poor thing."

"We were so close, I felt like she was me and I was her. That's why I'm in group. Because in a way, I *did* succumb to suicide."

I squeeze out a tear.

***

That's not how it happened at all.

Well, not exactly. It was our mother who found her. I knew Jessie was there, suspended in the basement by the washer and drier. I told her that would be the best if, "You know, if you were really to do it. Which you won't."

"Of course not," she agreed. "But why there?"

"Because of the door that leads to the garage. The EMTs, or whoever it is that shows up in such cases, would just have to cut you down, and take you discretely out back. No big scene out the front door, no neighbors standing around, gawking."

Though she'd once liked to be out with her friends to escape our mother's wrath, as her depression increased Jessie became a recluse. And shy. She hid her face behind veils of long, blonde hair, avoided eye contact, and basically didn't want to be seen at all. That's how I knew the idea of discretely slipping out the back door would appeal to her.

"I know it's kind of mean," she said, "but I'd want her to find me. To see what she did to me. Maybe then she'd be sorry."

I nodded. "I bet she would."

"Do you think it hurts?" Jesse asked.

"No more than the day-to-day pain of our miserable existence," I mumbled, picking at my fingernails.

That night, I gave her some poetry to read. The Keats bit about easeful death, hemlock and dissolving. *Ode to a Nightingale*, it's called. "Tender is the night," and its undying question, "Do I wake, or do I sleep?"

As predicted, Jessie chose sleep.

She didn't say to goodbye to me, but somehow when I woke the next morning – laundry day – I knew that she'd done it.

Mom's scream confirmed it.

I snuggled deeper into my bed, brought the covers over my ears, and pretended to be still asleep when she came flying into my room, frantic.

Not long after that, I reconnected with my dad, left the nest, and never saw my mother again.

* * *

My coffee's grown cold. The cinnamon has left an oily film on top.

Donna is holding me. She begins to kiss me. Here it comes – the pity sex. She feels sorry for me. Everything is going as planned.

I return her kisses, gazing gratefully at her through my tears. Pretty soon, robes are opening, and we're stumbling toward the bedroom.

I pin her down, and am rougher than she's used to. It's all a blur, really. But it feels good and it's a physical manifestation of my power over her. Of my power in admitting that I have a sister who died by her own hand. Next, I'll tell Donna about Jasmine. And my ex-husband, Stiles. He was so distraught after the divorce... it couldn't be helped.

Afterward, Donna gets up and goes to the kitchen to wash the breakfast dishes.

I head for the W.C. to freshen up. When I enter, I see the bathtub is full. There are bubbles on top, but I could swear I see a figure. I look a little closer.

No, there's no one in there.

"Donna?" I call out. "Do you want me to drain the tub?"

She comes to the doorway. "What do you mean?"

"Didn't you take a bath earlier?"

She looks into the room. "No. What are you talking about?"

I turn, following her gaze.

The tub is empty. And bone dry.

"Oh, sorry," I say, grinning sheepishly.

Donna shrugs. She turns and heads back into the kitchen.

I take a step closer to the tub. It *is* dry.

But there's steam on the window above. Written in the steam are the words, "Thank you."

I'll never forget those words. That was the last thing Jasmine ever said to me.

There's a great power in knowing someone's last words. Jessie's were "I love you," (written). Jasmine's were "Thank you" (spoken). Stiles' were "I can't live without you" (written).

I wonder what Donna's will be?

* * *

It's a quiet night at work. We only had one client, and she wasn't mine. So, I'm here in my office, looking through some of the new acquisitions. I've put on a record by The Velvet Underground, I have my coffee percolating, and I'm ready for the next several hours.

There are four crates on the floor. I'm opening them one by one. It's my job to catalogue and authenticate the treasures inside. It's going to take a week or so, but I don't mind.

This exhibit will be called *Spoils of War*. It's all the best stuff plundered from the biggest battles in history. One box contains various Viking pillage. Another one has armor from the War of the Roses. There're dolls from Dresden, and massive jewels from Iraq.

One object I can't stop staring at is Cleopatra's hand mirror. Made of thin bronze, so light and shiny it reflects almost as well as glass and silver, it's backed by enamel with an inlaid serpent design. The handle is made of wood and ivory. When the Romans sacked her palace, they took everything.

I look at my face in the mirror and imagine the Queen of the Nile herself looking into that exact same surface. Did she give herself a final once-over before taking her own life? I like to think that she did, and was satisfied with her beauty.

Just as I'm about to set the mirror aside, I see a streak pass behind me.

I turn. "Hello?"

No reply. I'm alone in the office.

Of course. Silly me.

But just to be sure, I hold the mirror up again, and search the periphery of its dark gleam. I think I see... No, *for sure* I see an indistinct figure huddled in the far corner of my office. I turn to look.

It's gone.

Tentatively, I raise the mirror again. There she is. It's Jasmine, nude and dripping wet. She sees that I see her. Jasmine's mouth moves, but I hear nothing.

I drop the mirror with a clang. Take a deep breath.

I should go home; I'm too tired.

But the night's work has only begun and I am no quitter.

I place the mirror back in its box, and I pick up a doll from Dresden. She certainly looks authentic. She's a bit burnt on one hand, and there's a reddish mark across her neck where the enamel was worn away – probably from a little girl carrying her around by the throat. But her shaped porcelain hair is perfect. Bright golden blonde, the color of sunflowers. She's got a slight, rosebud smile. Her eyes are blue.

No, wait. "Light blue," I write in my notations.

The record skips. I turn to look at the player, somewhat annoyed. Someone's been playing my records without permission. I take immense pride in my vinyl, and there isn't a single scratch on any track. The needle jumps again, placing itself perfectly at the beginning of *Pale Blue Eyes*.

I shake my head, annoyed. I turn back to my notations, only to find that I didn't write "light blue," to describe the doll's painted eyes – I wrote, "pale blue."

I glance over at the doll. I stare. It looks an awful lot like my sister. But no. It's just a doll, handmade, burnt, and stolen back in the blitzkrieg. Just a coincidence. Still, her face taunts me.

Linger on…
The doll's lips move.

No. It's just shadow-play.

I look for the source of the shadow, and see it. *Just* the shadow. Nothing casting it.

But I know Stiles' shape. There's a fluidness to the head, a… drippiness, from where he shot himself. I can't look away.

The volume on the record player suddenly increases. It's so loud. Then louder still. Somewhere, between Lou Reed's voice, the guitar and the bass, I hear whispers. "I love you. Thank you. I can't live without you."

Finally, I tear my gaze from the shadow.

I take a seat at my desk. A deep breath. A sip of cold coffee.

Then I see the icepick, and the mallet.

"How did you get here?" I stupidly ask the inanimate objects. Then again, how inanimate can they be, if they somehow got themselves out of the Chamber of Curses and onto my desk?

* * *

That was a strange night. But things have gotten stranger still. The icepick and the mallet wait for me everywhere, now. At home. In my car. At restaurants and bars. On my nightstand.

I can't help but wonder… should I use them? I want to. There's an almost overwhelming need to see what would happen. Will the nightmares go away if I do? What if I do it wrong? What if I kill myself?

"Do I wake, or do I sleep?"

FISHING WITH GRANDPA

By Darren Gordon Smith

"So, where exactly *is* this place?" She looked over at Sierra, whose hands were shaking at the steering wheel as the car's suspension bounced and bobbled down the gravelly road.

"It's just another half hour or so," Sierra said. It had already been at least that long since the girls exited the one-lane country road and opened the rusty metal gate to enter the private property. "C'mon Emily, we're going to have fun at the cottage. There's a big pool, Jacuzzi, ping pong table, tennis court. There's even a lake."

"Wait a minute – your family even has their own *lake?*" Emily figured her roomie was as rich as just about everybody else but her at their school, however, she had no idea that Sierra was *that* loaded.

"Yeah, though it's hardly one of the biggest lakes around here. Still it'll be relaxing – and quiet. Anyway, would you rather be spending Spring Break at a private lake, or with all the drunk, topless bimbos in Daytona?"

Emily laughed. Last Spring Break, in her freshman year, was spent waitressing at an Upper East Side bar filled drunk bros *and* topless bimbos. The idea that she'd even have the money to vacation in Florida when tuition at NYU was through the roof, was ludicrous. She figured she'd be lucky just to be able to earn enough scratch to fly home to L.A. for her mom's 50th birthday when spring semester was over. Her eyes fixated on a hawk (or was it a turkey buzzard?) hovering up ahead. "Yes, Si, I'd a million times rather be here in this beautiful countryside than anywhere else."

"Ha! I thought you said being out in the country gave you the creeps." Sierra was always ribbing Emily about being such a city girl. "Me, I used to spend just about every summer out here when I was little. Some of my best times were hanging by the lake and going fishing with my grandpa."

"That must have been nice," said Emily, thinking about her own grandparents who had died when she was a kid. "Is your grandfather still alive?"

"Oh, yeah, is he ever!" Sierra laughed. "He's out of the country right now, so it's a shame you won't meet him – he loves strawberry blondes like you! But he usually comes here at the start of summer and spends a few weeks here. He's the one who owns all this, by the way."

Emily looked around with awe as the road veered into a dense grove of white bark birch trees. A deer ambled its way across the road, so Sierra slowed the VW. "It's peaceful here, isn't it?" she said. "If it were me, I'd live out here all the time. But, like I said, it's my grandpa's. You know, my mom and me, we don't have any more money than you do. In fact, if it weren't for Grandpa paying for my schooling, I'd be doing work study, just like you."

"Wow, Si, I never knew that you weren't a one-percenter. Still, it's nice that your grandpa is so generous."

Sierra laughed in a way that Emily couldn't tell whether she was being sarcastic or bitter. "Yeah, well he's worth gazillions so he can afford to be generous. Wait, didn't I tell you? My grandpa is Rhys Weedham."

Em didn't know what to say, other than: "I'm sorry, Si, who is Reed Wheaton?"

"*Rhys Weedham.* Some people don't know him by name, but of course they know the band, Manifest Destiny."

"I think I may have heard of them." Emily recalled that her dad used to be into all those old rock groups; The Kinks, Traffic, Procol Harum. She remembered he had a couple Manifest Destiny CDs too. That was before Em's parents split up and her dad moved to Texas to become an asshole. "They're an English band, right?"

"Of course! Wait, Em, I can't believe you don't know really know who they are! *Get With the Word? Donut Hole Rockin' Roll? Sinner's Revenge? All My Women Better be True?* Come on, you know *Snake & Kidney Pie,* right?"

Emily shook her head. "Sorry, I guess I'm as out of it as all the other pre-meds in our dorm."

"No, no, Em, don't feel bad. It's actually kind of cool that you don't know them. Most people, when I tell them that my grandpa's the bass player and founding member of Manifest Destiny, almost all the guys are like, 'No shit? Can I meet him? Can you give him my band's demo?' Girls are about the same when I tell them, but then a lot of them also ask, 'Is he, you know, single?'"

"Single? Wait, how old is your grandfather?"

"He just turned 68 this year. I *know*, it's crazy, girls our age wanting to date him. But then, Donald Trump has dated women about a third his age, so go figure. Of course it has nothing to do with the money, right? Anyway, you can see that's why I don't usually talk about my famous gramps. I love him and am proud of him, of course. I mean, he's so talented. Kind of a visionary, I guess you could say." Sierra's voice turned to a conspiratorial whisper. "But Grandpa is also, well, I'm not trying to be ungrateful – and please do not breathe a word of this to anyone – he's a spoiled child. Go figure, he's been rich and famous since he was a teenager. I mean, the guy once held up a sold-out crowd at Madison Square Garden for two hours until he got his special steak and kidney pie shipped to him and fed to him by his top five groupies."

"He actually made the entire crowd wait before he got his food?"

Sierra nodded. "And, he's got several generations of an entourage, and, Jesus, how that posse that kisses his royal rock star ass. He lives in a bubble – constantly touring around the world in royal style, and getting everything he wants whenever he wants it. My mom said when she was growing up she barely knew him. Even on the rare occasions that he was home, rather than spending time with his daughter or wife, he'd spend the whole time in his basement studio, saying he had to get his musical ya-yas out."

"*Ya-yas*? I love that."

Sierra grinned. "Not all of those ya-yas were musical, either. I got to hand to him, for being as old as he is, he's still a sexual dynamo."

"How would *you* know that?"

"That's according to his latest wife. And my grandmother, who was his third or fourth wife, I forget, said that he had enough sexual energy to satisfy a stable of lovers. And that's what he did, he had a stable even when they were married. Still does, the horn dog. That's how come he has 14 kids with eight different women – and why I'm one of his – I think he's got 33 grandchildren, so far. The only cool part is that the mothers of all his children represent all races and varying ethnicities so we've got a frickin' United Nations of Weedham spawn around the world. He was an equal opportunity exploiter, like my grandma always says. Just last year, a sex tape of him making it with two identically tanned and waxed Brazilians was all over the Web. Rather than be embarrassed about the video, he actually told TMZ that his lifetime goal is to get on Maxim Magazine's list of Top 10 Living Sex Legends. I swear the man's 68 going on 18."

"So he's going through some sort of late-midlife crisis?"

"Em, my grandpa never reached midlife – emotionally or mentally - to ever even *have* a midlife crisis! He's always had a steady supply of mostly young women around to satisfy his needs. And I mean   *young* – his last three girlfriends have been our age."

Emily made a face. "I'm sorry, Si, I don't even know your granddad, but a 68 year old guy with a 20 year old? That's just gross."

Sierra looked a little offended. "Well, apparently *they* don't think so. Even some of my girlfriends are flattered by his attention. He can be pretty charming. And persistent. So when he gets fixated on some woman, for the evening, for the month, whatever, he almost always gets what he wants. And I'm not talking by force, obviously. We're talking persuasion, like, 'Oh, I'll give you some spending money, or I'll pay your rent,' whatever. At least he's good on his promises, that's to his credit. I just hate his mind games, and him always threatening to not pay my tuition unless he gets me to go along with whatever stupid thing he wants."

"Like what?" Just as Em said that, she was sorry, for she saw the pained look that came across her friend's face.

"Well, like I had this best friend since grade school, Keira, and last summer I was hanging with her up at the cottage. But then Old Man Weedham ogles her while we're lying by the pool and starts coming on to her. I thought she'd be disgusted, but Keira was flattered. I was disgusted, of course. I took him aside and we quarreled and then he said, 'Well, if you don't like the fact that I express my sexual appetite whenever the hell I please, you can get the fuck out of here. And by the way, forget about going back to college 'cause I ain't paying for it'."

"So I suppose you couldn't really say anything about him and your friend after that?"

"That's right. He gave Keira his freaky look and said, 'I want you.' Don't ask me how that line worked, but she went upstairs with him and for the rest of the summer he was fucking her brains out. Almost literally, too, 'cause she started acting like a ditz around him. I was angry for a while, but we worked it out. Now, Grandpa is paying all her expenses at Amherst. All Keira's got to do is handle a conjugal visit now and again."

Just as Emily was mulling over whether she could ever have sex with a man over 30, or indeed, whether she'd ever have sex again after her college boyfriend dumped her last semester, they drove up the circular driveway to approach The House.

This was no quaint, little summer cottage. This was a baronial estate, a mansion with rock star hippie vibe - a rustic mismatch of log cabin and Haight Ashbury Victorian style bay windows and ornate glass, all supersized; a kind of Jay Gatsby meets Grizzly Adams playhouse. A bronze sculpture of an ample bosomed nude stood over the porch like a hood ornament on a pornographer's town car. This was going to be quite an experience! Em couldn't wait to tell her mom about it, but *dammit,* her cellphone died on the way and she left her charger at home.

"Oh, look," said Sierra.

"What is it?"

"Look over there, it's Grandpa's helicopter. He must be here, probably inside."

As if on cue, two men opened the tall front doors and then The Man, The Legend, swaggered between them and came out to greet the girls. He had a shit-eating grin and gave his granddaughter a big hug. "Babe, it's great to see you. Our tour ended a few shows early so I wanted to get out here and relax as soon as I could. Your mum said you'd be here and bringing a guest."

He turned to Emily. "I recognize you from the photos, you must be Sierra's roommate," he gave her a friendly smile and extended his hand to her. "My name is Rhys."

"Oh, uh, pleased to meet you." The man didn't seem to be the asshole she'd pictured in her mind. Maybe the guy's a letch but at least he's charming, almost self-effacing. And he didn't look nearly as old as she'd imagined he'd be. Older, of course, but more like maybe mid-40s. Like Sierra, he had long, dark, wavy hair, which must be dyed she thought, but maybe not. He wasn't all out of shape, either. As silly as it seemed for him to be wearing all leather on this sunny spring day, Em could see that he was trim for a man his age, tall and maybe even a little too skinny.

The Rock Star said, "Much obliged, Sierra, for bringing this lovely creature here, she's even prettier in person." He winked at Emily.

"You're welcome grandpa," replied Sierra. "You'll have to tell me all about your tour! Weren't you in Australia?"

"There and New Zealand, Indonesia, the Philippines, Thailand."

"I've always wanted to go to Thailand," said Emily. "Do you have a lot of fans there?"

Rhys made a big belly laugh. "You might say that, my dear Emily. Thailand wasn't part of the tour, though. I just went for, let's just say, personal reasons." He winked at Sierra. "By the way, you're going to have a new uncle or aunt in six months. From Phuket."

Rhys had one of his lackeys take Emily's bags and show her to her room. Before leaving, the lackey gave her two freshly baked chocolate chip cookies. This was like one of those 5-star hotels that she'd only read about. The cookies smelled and tasted delicious! Chocolatey, warm, and slightly gooey, like some irresistible protoplasm, overloading her salivary glands with each crumbly bite.

Suddenly, there was a knock on the door.

It was Sierra. "I've got some really good news, Em."

"Spit it out."

"Grandpa likes you."

"Well that's nice; he seemed like a pretty cool, down-to-earth guy."

"No. I mean he REALLY likes you. As in, you know, he *wants* you. Is that great? Play your cards right, and you'll never have to take out another student loan again!"

About Darren Gordon Smith

What can I say about Darren Gordon Smith that hasn't already been said by the City of Seward Police Department?

Well, there are a few things they (and you) may not know. Darren and I met in Toronto, Canada in 2007 on the set of *Repo! The Genetic Opera*, a feature horror musical film he was producing along with his writing partner Terrance Zdunich and director Darren Lynn Bousman. I have since remained close with all three men (insert your own screw-in-a-lightbulb joke here) but since this is "About Darren Gordon Smith," let's get back to him, shall we?

DGS is one of the funniest, smartest, most quirkily intellectual and multitalented persons on the planet. He's the Froot to my Loop; the epic to my fail; the 43:46 Jethro Tull *Thick As A Brick* to my John Cage *4'33"*; he's the lion standing alone to my tadpole in a jar. And he knows how to play the keytar, for goshsakes!

I picture DGS in an alternate reality as a Bob Newhart style standup, mind unbuttoned. Or as a serial killer (he does have three names, after all. Wait. So do I. Hm…) who specializes in slaying only those who don't like *American Psycho* and sorbet. Maybe in the multiverse, he's a mash-up of Stephen Hawking and Stephen Stills with an earthshattering guitar-string theory about Buffalo Springfield.

But in *this* world Darren is a filmmaker, composer, writer, artist and diehard Peter Lemongello fan. Oh, and he's also an attorney at law. In short: He's a sextuple threat!

[For photographic evidence of said keytar prowess, visit Darren's home on the web: DarrenGordonSmith.com]

About Staci Layne Wilson

Many of you are too young to remember the fall of '07, a dark time when the world seemed gripped by disease, desperation, and despair. Like other brave Americans, I escaped to Toronto to be on the set of

Repo. There, I met Staci Layne Wilson, another temporary expat. Staci was implacable, imperturbable – and thoroughly unflappable. She claimed to be there on a "junket" but refused to elaborate.

I'll never forget her streak of blue hair, which sparkled like Technicolor in that otherwise monochromatic era. And a necklace containing (trigger warning here, folks) mystical runes. Spooky runes. Prehistoric symbols that are now believed to have been used long ago by a small tribe known as Led Zeppelin IV. The symbols apparently signify satanic mud shark baths and death from 40 shots of vodka.

To show Staci that I was on to her, I quoted St. Robert o' Plant, "I'm waiting for the angels of Avalon." She did not respond with "Waiting for the Eastern glow," as I had expected. Like I said, the woman was, and still is, unflappable. (Maybe she didn't hear me.)

Still, I knew we had a connection, an understanding. An understanding that she would continue to develop her already accomplished skills as a writer, filmmaker, artist, journalist, and TV host. And, over the past eight years I've known her, that's exactly what she did.

As 'matter of fact, if Dos Equis had a Most Interesting Woman in the World, she'd be it. But without the pretentious accent. I'm mean, fuck me, but the girl's done it all: trained animals, traveled the world in seven seas, jawboned with the late Ray

Manzarek, and mysteriously collected merry-go-round ponies.

A few weeks ago – eons in Facebook time – Staci posted, "I never thought I'd be doing this." I don't even remember what "this" was, but I remember thinking, whatever it is, I could definitely imagine Staci doing it. Thank God my keytar's gone. If she got her hands on that thing, I have no doubt that she'd soon be "Safety Dancing" circles around me. And she'd probably get the thing impounded by Australian's strict animal control laws for playing a keytar like an animal.

One might say that she's Ringo to my Pete Best, Jekyll to my Hyde, the two good Godfather films to my Godfather III, her S.A.G. to my scab, her Pulitzer to my Nobel Booby Prize, her Howitzer to my hoe, her browser (no matter what she has) to my Bing, my coyote to her roadrunner, her death-side embrace by the sweet arms of Jesus, to my eternal damnation in Hell. She's the Great Communicator, The Great Santini, and The Big Lebowski, all rolled up into one.

[Staci's home on the web can be found at: StaciLayneWilson.com]